To Keep an Emerald Rose

A BOUND BY FLAME NOVELLA

ELAYNA R. GALLEA

To all my fellow dragon lovers.
This one's for you.

CHAPTER 1

Stereotypes, Handsome Intruders, and Very Bad Days

Octavia Ashbloom was slowly going mad. Lying back with her long, black, curly hair fanned out around her like a dark angel, she stared at the ceiling. The incessant *pitter-patter* of rain hitting the shingles was inescapable, loud, and horribly annoying. The walls of this too-small shack were closing in on her.

She groaned, dropping her face into her hands. Drop by drop, minute by minute, hour by hour, the rain was chipping away at her sanity... and there wasn't much there to begin with.

Every time the thunder roared like an infuriated dragon, the paper-thin walls shook. Her heart sped up, and her lungs tightened to the point of pain. She was surprised the roof was still holding on.

She'd been okay the first few days, but the storm had been going on for a week. Who knew rain could be so devastating? Day and night, the torrential deluge continued. At this point, sleep was a distant memory. Every time Octavia closed her eyes and tried to rest, the storm picked up again.

She was exhausted and cranky. Very, very cranky. Her grandma Gertrude used to call this "burn the house down" cranky. That was a fair assessment. Anger in their kind usually resulted in a few fires.

1

Octavia had never understood what her grandmother was talking about until this week. Everything was too loud, too sharp, too irritating. She had never considered herself particularly inclined to murder, having been raised with the belief that excessive violence was usually unnecessary, but at this point, she would kill someone if it got her out of this mess.

She could already hear the village gossips, gathering around the well as they shared the daily news.

"Did you hear what Octavia Ashbloom did?" someone, probably the chatterbox Millicent Firebreath, would ask.

"That failed messenger? What has she done now?" another busybody—likely one of the Ignis sisters, they were so nosy—would reply.

"She murdered someone just to get out of a storm. Can you imagine? What kind of dragon shifter doesn't like the rain?"

The gossips would titter and gasp, but no one would be surprised. After all, Octavia wasn't exactly adored by the members of her village. They would just assume her temper got the best of her.

Talk about stereotypes. People always assumed that dragon shifters lived in a state of continual anger, but that wasn't the case. They just had shorter tempers and tended to set things on fire on a regular basis.

It was usually an accident.

Thunder boomed outside, and Octavia pressed her hands against her ears.

"Make it stop," she moaned, pleading to whatever gods might be listening.

She loved being a dragon shifter—not that she had a choice in the matter since she was born that way—but sometimes, the extra-sensitive hearing and powerful sense of smell became too much for her to handle. Each drop of water pelting the roof was like a needle being shoved beneath her skin.

As if mocking her pleas, another boom of thunder rolled over the forest, and the rain picked up.

"Why is this my life?" Octavia grumbled.

No one answered. Of course not. She was the only one there.

Seven days ago, Octavia had been hiking through the endless woods when the storm had moved in. Green, angry clouds had swirled in the sky. The temperature, which had been a comfortable summer heat, dropped. Silence fell on the forest minutes before the tempest began.

The rain was so bad it was as though Nontia, the goddess of the sea, was angry with the land and wanted to drown all living creatures. She had certainly put forth a valiant effort.

By the time Octavia had stumbled upon this shack, the rain had soaked through her tunic and leggings. Despite her efforts to protect her belongings, even her messenger bag had been water-logged.

She'd found shelter inside and had been here ever since.

It had been a long week. All she had were trail rations, a small water bottle, and her own miserable company.

During that time, Octavia had learned two things.

First, collecting and drinking rainwater was unpleasant on the best of days. Doing so when you were trapped in a small hunter's shack in the middle of the gods-damned wild with no company to talk to and four tiny walls to look at was even worse.

Second, and probably more importantly, Octavia was terrible company when she was grumpy, wet, and alone. If she survived this, she would have to do some introspection to determine what, exactly, that said about her.

She pushed herself to a sitting position on the bed/chair/table/only-piece-of-furniture in the entire shack and shook her head. "This is what you get for volunteering to make a delivery to Winifred Black." She kicked her bag, which was now dry and sitting at her feet. "Regaining your reputation as an honorable messenger won't help much if you're dead."

Now, Octavia was so far gone that she was carrying on conversations with herself.

Even worse? She paused as though she was waiting for an answer.

It did not come.

Obviously.

Octavia's dragon was silent, and there was no one else to talk to. The fiery creature that shared the messenger's skin was just as upset with her as the Elders. The dragon was a petulant beast, taking out its anger on Octavia by ignoring her completely.

How many days could someone be trapped in a small space without losing their mind completely?

Right now, Octavia was fairly certain the answer was less than seven.

If the Elders hadn't insisted that Octavia take this journey on foot as part of her penance, she could have been there and back by now. But no, she wasn't allowed to shift. Before she left, the Elders assured her they would know if she freed her dragon before it was time. A Fortune Elf would be Watching her path at all times.

Gods.

Screw up one delivery soon after Maturing, and all of a sudden, it's "Octavia can't be trusted," "Octavia is a bad messenger," and "Octavia is the worst dragon shifter ever to live in the Rose Empire."

Okay, she might have made that last one up, but the picture was clear, right?

Listen, it wasn't even like Octavia killed anyone. She wasn't a secret assassin or anything insanely interesting like that. She just... accidentally set fire to a letter she was supposed to deliver to the Empress herself and was at least partially responsible for throwing the Empire into the War of Iron Teeth against the fae.

Look, everyone made mistakes every once in a while.

Fifty-five years later, Octavia was still trying to make it up to the Elders. It was said that out of all the species that lived in the Rose Empire—dragons, elves, vampires, witches, werewolves, shifters, mermaids, and humans—dragons held onto grudges the longest.

Octavia was living proof of that.

It wasn't like she'd lost control of her dragon and given into the beast's primal instincts, turning into a draken. Now, *that* would be bad.

Unfortunately for Octavia, the Elders disagreed. That was how she found herself traveling on foot through dark forests and over mountains to deliver a package. Hopefully, by accomplishing her mission, Octavia would finally find a way back into her community's good graces once and for all.

Being the least trusted member of her tight-knit community sucked. Octavia was regularly left out of events, and most members of Firefall Village barely spoke to her.

Unfortunately for her, the rain had set her way behind schedule. At this rate, it would take her at least a month to make it to the Indigo Coast. At least once she completed her delivery, she had clearance to shift and fly home. Thank Kydona, the mother goddess, for small mercies.

Settling her back against the wall—it wasn't like there was anywhere else to go—Octavia closed her eyes.

They were shut for less than a minute before a branch cracked outside.

Her eyes flung open.

Another *snap*, this one louder.

Her skin crawled as she looked around the shack for a weapon. Sadly, an armory hadn't miraculously appeared. Her options were limited to her walking stick and the very small dagger tucked in her boot.

Rising from the bed, Octavia grabbed the stick and took a deep breath. She could do this. She was a Mature dragon shifter in the prime of her life—an alpha creature in a forest full of tiny squirrels and raccoons. Dragon shifters dominated the food chain in the Rose Empire, which was why everyone feared them.

It's probably nothing, Octavia reasoned with herself.

Still, she couldn't shake the feeling that someone was out there.

Tightening her grip on her walking stick, she wrenched the door open.

"Aha!" Octavia yelled, brandishing her very impressive weapon as she battled her attacker. She was a fierce dragon shifter. A warrior. Her senses were strong. She would destroy...

The wind.

Her attacker was the wind. Unsurprisingly, it pushed her around, and her strikes were useless. She was average-sized for a dragon shifter and a little leaner than most.

No one was there.

Within seconds of leaving the safety of her shack, Octavia was drenched. The summer rain soaked through her tunic and trousers as though they were nothing but sheets of parchment. They stuck to her frame as she circled the shack as quickly as she could manage. The rain caused her once-injured-and-never-quite-properly-healed ankle to burn, but she didn't see anything amiss.

Damn it. Seven days and Octavia had officially lost her mind. Dragon shifters were supposed to have extraordinary senses, not get tricked by the wind. Thank the gods, none of the villagers were here to witness her embarrassment. If they'd seen her, she would never have lived it down.

Sighing, she trudged back inside the shack. The door swung open with ease, and she shook off the rain, planning on taking a well-deserved nap and elevating her foot after such strenuous activity.

Except...

Her empty shack wasn't so empty anymore.

The good news was that Octavia hadn't gone completely mad, and her senses were still functioning.

The bad news—and she could not emphasize bad enough—was that she was no longer alone.

This might not have been extremely clear yet, but Octavia was awkward and had trouble around others.

Unbelievable, right?

A lithe, tall intruder wearing a black cloak had his back to

Octavia as he rifled through a bag. *Her* bag. As if he owned the place.

To be clear, Octavia didn't either, but she had gotten here first. That meant something.

Anger was a blazing fire as it surged through Octavia, and her dragon unfurled. The beast maintained its silence, but Octavia felt her watching.

Shifting her grip on the walking stick, the dragon shifter tried to infuse her voice with as much strength as possible. "Excuse me? Who the fuck are you, and what do you think you're doing?"

The intruder straightened. His shoulders came together, and he dropped Octavia's bag on the ground before turning around.

Octavia's jaw dropped open. Good gods. Never in her entire life had she seen anyone so... so... perfect.

The intruder's wavy hair was somewhere between red and brown, and it dusted the back of his neck. His skin was tanned and freckled, a testament to countless hours spent in the sun. His entire body was sculpted and muscular. His brown eyes were sharp and wide, studying her intently. Two rounded ears were visible beneath his hair, but she couldn't tell what kind of being he was. Human, shifter, or witch...

Whatever. It really didn't matter. What was more important were the solid lines of his clenched jaw and his handsome face that had Octavia squeezing her thighs at the sight.

How embarrassing. He could have been there to kill her, and she was dreaming about how his lips would taste.

Not her finest moment.

Snap out of it, the dragon snarled.

Great. *Now*, the dragon was talking. Couldn't she have pipped up a few hours ago when the shifter was questioning her sanity?

Octavia couldn't talk to the dragon right now. She had an intruder to contend with. Honestly, looking as good as this man did should be illegal. Maybe it was. There were so many laws in the Rose Empire that it was difficult to keep track of them all.

Of all the Empresses the Rose Empire had had—eleven in total

—the current one was the most violent. Rumors circulated in the dark corners of taverns about her laws. The Emerald Empress had supposedly banned her subjects from wearing jewel-toned colors in her presence upon the threat of disembowelment and death. Speaking out of turn in her court? Disembowelment and death. Talking to a fae from across the Indigo Ocean? Disembowelment and death.

Talk about an extreme lack of creativity.

Still, a summons to the Emerald Palace would have even the most battle-hardened Death Elves quaking in their boots. The gods help whatever poor male would be roped into marrying the Emerald Empress after the Marriage Games next year.

"Why are you staring at me?" the rude intruder asked, drawing Octavia out of her thoughts.

She blinked, shaken by the fact that she'd allowed her mind to wander during such an inopportune moment. "Answer my questions first!"

A smirk danced on the intruder's lips, and his hand dropped to his side. He pulled back his cloak just enough to display the very shiny, very large sword hanging at his hip.

Damn it all.

The insanely attractive intruder had a scary weapon. Octavia's walking stick was no match for that.

It was official. This would be a very bad day.

CHAPTER 2

Death by Sword was Better than Being Struck by Lightning

"My name's Octavia," the dragon shifter said, recognizing that she was no match against the intruder. At least, not in here. Out there, in her shifted form, it would be a different story.

She'd like to see him wave that sword at her when her dragon was loose. Limp or not, the creature living beneath her skin was massive.

At that exact same moment, thunder rumbled through the sky, and the rain picked up even more. Octavia glanced behind her at the very wet forest, and then she looked inside the shack. Neither option was particularly delightful, but seeing as how she did not want to be struck by lightning, she moved inside. If she had to pick a way to die, death by sword seemed like the better option.

She did keep the door open, though. After all, she had a modicum of preservation instincts.

The intruder dipped into a courtly bow, which was honestly a miracle considering the cramped quarters. Between the two of them, there was barely a foot of unoccupied space in the shack. "It's a pleasure to meet you, Lady Octavia."

Her eyes narrowed. Lady, she was not. Dragon shifters generally kept to themselves, as most of the Rose Empire didn't exactly trust them. It could have been because of the enormous fire-breathing beasts residing within the shifters, or maybe it was their less-than-delightful temperaments. Dragons tended to be an angry, possessive group and didn't play well with others.

Still, Octavia didn't correct the man. Call her crazy, but it was nice to hear someone talk about her without the scorn and ridicule that typically accompanied interactions with her fellow villagers.

"Thank you," Octavia said after a moment. "And you are..."

Her voice trailed off as she waited for him to answer.

The intruder raised one of those stupidly perfect brown brows. The dazzling smile he sent her way made her insides twist in a way that was most unbecoming of a messenger trying not to get herself skewered by the aforementioned intruder. "Flynn Tririver, at your service, my lady."

"And what, pray tell, are you doing here, Flynn?" she asked, trying to sound authoritative.

Based on the smirk still dancing on his face, it wasn't working. "I'm seeking shelter from the storm," he said as though it was obvious.

All his tone did was make her more frustrated. The ache in her ankle wasn't helping matters either. Leaning on her walking stick, Octavia snapped, "I gathered as much. I meant here, in the forest."

"I'm looking for something," was his vague reply.

Suspicion flared within the dragon shifter, and her eyes narrowed. "You're looking for something in the middle of the never-ending forest?"

With the exception of a few cities scattered across the massive continent, the Rose Empire was largely made up of forests and mountains. There were, of course, slight variations. In the north, past the Koln Mountains, the mountains and forests were covered in snow. On the western plains, the land was relatively flat, but trees still abounded. In the south, the mountains were made of sand.

Most dragon shifters were well-traveled throughout the continent, their deliveries taking them all over the place. Even though

Octavia had been grounded before she could get much traveling in, she'd heard plenty of stories about the world in which they lived.

No one crossed the Indigo Ocean, though. The fae were not kind, and they were not to be dealt with. They remained on their side of the Obsidian Coast, and the citizens of the Rose Empire stayed away.

Flynn nodded. "Yes, I am."

Octavia glared at the intruder, giving him her best, *I don't believe you,* look. Unfortunately, she wasn't sure it worked because those brown eyes laughed at her.

Then she realized something. She was soaked from her earlier excursion, but there wasn't a single drop of water on Flynn. Her nostrils flared, and she adjusted her grip on the walking stick, taking weight off her ankle. "Why aren't you wet?"

Flynn looked down at his clothes, then back up again. "Oh, this?" he shrugged, but there was a twinkle in his stupid eyes. "I shielded myself. The rain doesn't bother me."

That skill was... surprisingly useful. She could have used that a week ago.

But now she had a hint about this mysterious stranger.

"You're a witch?" she asked, unable to hide the intrigue in her voice.

He canted his head, a lock of his hair falling ruggedly over his forehead. "That I am, my lady."

How utterly fascinating. Octavia had never met a witch before. The other species who lived in the Rose Empire didn't exactly spend a lot of time with dragon shifters.

Maybe a witch could've healed her ankle properly after her fall. Octavia had tumbled out of a tree as a child, and since she hadn't been Mature, her foot had never properly healed. She had learned to live with it, though. The injury didn't mean she was different from anyone else. She just walked a little slower than others.

"What are you good at?" Leaning on her walking stick, Octavia threw propriety aside for the sake of curiosity and new acquaintances.

Besides, if Flynn were going to kill her, he'd probably have done it by now. Villains with murderous intentions didn't go around holding conversations first with the women they intended to decapitate, right?

Octavia didn't think so.

She wasn't letting her guard down as much as accepting her situation.

Flynn raised a brow. "Well, if you must know, I've been told I'm an excellent kisser."

"What?" Octavia sputtered. Her heart pounded as the walls of this too-small shack seemed to mock her with their closeness. "I... What?"

How in Kydona's holy name did they get from magic to kissing? She had no idea, but now that he'd said it, she couldn't get the image of them locking lips out of her mind. The visual was all too clear, and by all the gods, it was *good*. She could visualize the whole scene, from how his slightly taller frame would lean over hers, crowding her space. His hands would come up and cup her jaw, gently but forcefully moving her into his favorite position before his mouth lowered and he...

Octavia's cheeks heated, and she shook her head. "I meant with your magic," she said a little too briskly.

She probably should've been more specific. She wouldn't make that mistake again. And now, as penance, she was stuck with the image of them kissing in her head. Even though she tried to banish the thought, it was surprisingly stuck in her mind. Her lips tingled, and she couldn't help but stare at his plump, kissable mouth. It wasn't like she'd never been kissed, but it had been some time since she'd had some... attention.

As if the witch could read Octavia's mind, he chuckled. "Apologies, Octavia. Perhaps you should've been a little clearer with your question."

"Maybe you should have been a little less obtuse," she retorted. The mix-up wasn't entirely her fault. *He* was the one who'd jumped to kissing.

A laugh was his only response. The booming sound filled the small cabin, and she was horrified to discover that she really liked it.

That only served to frustrate Octavia further. She glared at him. "Well? Will you tell me what kind of witchly magic you are good at?"

"I could," he said coyly, "or I could show you."

Her heart skipped a beat as his words echoed in her ears. What kind of things did he want to show her? She wasn't sure, and honestly, she didn't even know why she was still entertaining this conversation. She should insist he leave, taking his magic and his good looks with him, but she was curious and no longer alone. Octavia's mother, Yvette, Kydona be with her soul, always told her daughter her curiosity would get the better of her one day.

She was right.

Octavia nodded, attempting to be as nonchalant as possible despite the fact that her heart was now making a valiant effort to beat its way out of her chest. "Okay, show me."

Without warning, Flynn closed the distance between them. He reached for Octavia's hand, and she... let him take it.

A jolt ran through her at their first touch, but she didn't pull away. Yes, there was definitely something wrong with her. Octavia had always craved touch and enjoyed the safety of letting someone else hold her, but this felt different. More. The witch's hand on hers made her feel whole in a way she hadn't for decades.

Throwing caution to the wind, Octavia leaned into the handsome intruder's touch. It was not her finest moment, but she was having plenty of those today. She'd just chalk the entire meeting up to a bad decision when it finally ended.

Flynn made a sound of surprise, and then his grip tightened around her fingers. Did he feel it, too? She didn't ask.

The witch closed his eyes, and his lips moved silently. Sky blue ribbons left his hands. They swirled around them, and then, energy coursed through Octavia's veins. It was like she'd swallowed lightning, and it now lived within her. She widened her eyes. Blue sparks jumped off her skin, and a sheen of the same color surrounded them.

"What is this?" she asked in wonderment.

The witch's brown eyes opened and met hers. For a moment, everything else faded. The rain falling outside, the thunder, even the racing of her heart. It was just the two of them and the way he looked at her.

Who was this man that he made her feel this way?

As if he, too, realized they were staring at each other, Flynn cleared his throat and shrugged. "It's a shield. I'm partial to them, and the magic comes easily to me."

"It's beautiful," Octavia breathed. Her hand rose, and she caught a stray ribbon floating in the air around them. The magic sent a jolt through her, but it didn't disintegrate. Instead, it shimmered and seemed to do a little dance in the air.

Flynn smirked. "It likes you."

He spoke of his magic as though it were a living, breathing creature. As though his magic were an entity outside of himself like Octavia's dragon was to her.

The shifter opened her hand, and the ribbon twisted through her long fingers. It was soft and delicate, utterly unlike the witch who'd broken into her cabin.

Wait.

Octavia sucked in a breath. How could she have forgotten? Flynn wasn't just a handsome witch with fancy blue magic and a touch that sent tingles through her. He was the too-handsome-for-his-own-good stranger who'd broken into her tiny cabin and rummaged through her things.

Good gods, Octavia, she scolded herself and took a shaky step back. *At least try to keep your head on your shoulders.*

She had a mission to complete. A delivery to finish. What kind of messenger completely forgot about their task? A bad one. Octavia already had a record of screwing things up. She couldn't let things get any worse.

Flynn must have noticed the change in her because his eyes widened. "What's wrong?"

Octavia moved back, and her legs bumped against the bed. She bent, never removing her gaze from the witch, as she grabbed her upturned messenger bag. Sticking her hand inside, she felt around until the cool, smooth edges she sought met her fingertips.

Ashes and smoke, that was close. What would Octavia have done if she lost this? She couldn't return home to Firefall, that was certain. No one would have her back if she failed this mission. Then she'd be Octavia Ashbloom, twice failed messenger and eternal reject.

That could not happen. She wouldn't allow it.

Steeling her face, Octavia released the object and straightened. "What's wrong is that you're in my cabin, and I don't even know you."

He frowned as though he truly didn't understand the issue at hand. "I told you, my name's Flynn, and I'm a witch. What else is there to know?"

There were many things, but Octavia didn't have time for them. Shaking her head, she grabbed her walking stick. Her chest nearly brushed against Flynn's as she inched past him towards the door.

How come she hadn't realized how close they were standing? Was she so starved for any sort of attention that she had abandoned all illusions of common sense? Apparently so.

"It was... interesting to meet you," Octavia said, unwilling to lie. She'd be willing to bet half her hoard that this handsome witch would haunt her dreams tonight.

"Likewise." Flynn's brows furrowed. "Where are you—"

Choosing escape as the most expedient way out of what was rapidly becoming the strangest—and most titillating—experience of her entire life, Octavia turned and fled toward the open door. "Goodbye."

She was drenched the moment she stepped foot outside. Had the storm worsened? That was just her luck. Icy water pelted her from above. Curses that would have made any dragon shifter blush poured from Octavia's mouth as her muscles temporarily seized. If it weren't for the witch, she could've stayed dry. Now, that option was gone.

"Lady Octavia—" Flynn touched her arm, and those familiar sparks returned.

Shocked out of her stupor, Octavia yanked her arm away. "Leave me the hell alone!"

Holding her bag tight against her side with one hand and her walking stick with the other, she ran from Flynn.

Well.

Ran may have been a slight overstatement. Using her cane, she navigated through the wet woods as speedily as she dared. The last thing she needed was to turn her ankle again, force a shift, and fly away. The Elders really would never forgive her if that happened.

With every step on sodden leaves, every leap over small brooks, and every turn around trees, Octavia ran from the witch. She pumped her arms, her heart pounded, and her lungs tightened. This was exhausting and, quite frankly, horrid. Who exercised for fun? Running was awful. Octavia was sure her hip would bruise where the bag slammed into it, but she had to continue.

Once she finished this delivery, things would be different. She was determined to take up a sedentary lifestyle. Her lungs burned like tiny embers had taken up residency within them. Her heart hammered, and her boots were wet.

Was there anything worse than wet feet that squished with every step?

She didn't think so.

At least the witch was nowhere in sight. Hopefully, he'd gotten the hint—she'd certainly yelled loud enough—and he wouldn't be back. Still, she cursed that wretched, good-looking witch for forcing her out of her shack.

She'd been running for at least an hour before twilight set in. Night was falling, and she was wet, hungry, and alone in the forest.

Just fucking great.

Then, as if things couldn't get any worse, thunder boomed. Octavia shrieked as white lightning flashed across the sky. She darted beneath a tree, which was probably unwise but her first instinct, and she panted as the thunder rolled for what felt like the longest minute ever.

As she stood there, trembling, her mind decided this was the perfect moment to show her images of what she and Flynn could've been doing in the nice, dry cabin. Her brain was a horrible traitor. How dare it betray her in such a manner?

Images flashed through her mind of them kissing, ending up naked and in the only bed, sharing warmth.

Stop! Octavia wanted to smack her head against the tree.

This was wrong. The witch was bad. She couldn't be thinking about him. Besides, she'd lost him now and would never see him again.

Get it together, she chided herself. She'd never lusted after anyone like this before. What was wrong with her?

Leaving the shelter of the tree behind, Octavia slipped under branches, moved around trees, and hobbled over logs that definitely didn't count as real bridges. She needed to keep going. The sooner she got her delivery over with, the sooner she could return to Firefall.

That would solve all her problems.

The sun ceded its place in the sky to the moon as Octavia hurried east. Always east. Every so often, she felt like someone was watching her. Unease twisted her stomach, but every time she looked around, she didn't see anyone.

Clutching her bag, she ran even faster.

———

THE MOON HAD BEEN in the sky for several hours by the time Octavia's ankle forced her to stop. Each step sent fire running through her foot. She didn't want to sleep in the middle of the woods, though. The rain had let up a bit, but it was still a steady drizzle. Also, who knew what other kinds of animals were here?

A shelter was necessary.

Luckily, a small cavern up ahead caught her eye. It was out of the way and looked safe enough. Thanking Kydona for her small mercies, Octavia dragged her weary, sodden body over to the cave. She had just enough energy to quickly sweep the space for unwanted critters. She may have been a dragon shifter, but she hated mice just as much as the next person.

Thank the gods, other than a few stray pieces of dried grass, the cavern was empty. Octavia dropped to the ground and clutched her satchel. Exhaling, she extended her leg. Placing her throbbing ankle on top of the bag and stretching the walking stick across her lap, she closed her eyes.

She would sleep for a few hours, and then she'd—

"Why did you run from me?"

Octavia screamed.

CHAPTER 3
Disrupted Plans and Tempting Distractions

Her eyes flew open, and she met Flynn's brown gaze. "You," she snarled.

"I've seen drowned rats that look better than you." The infuriating, smug bastard was dry.

"Go away," Octavia snapped, waving her walking stick in his direction. "Find your own cave."

She was in no mood to deal with this witch who apparently couldn't take a hint. Not now. Maybe in the morning, when she was well-rested, and her ankle no longer felt like her mortal enemy, she could deal with him. But right now, he was just... too much. Too handsome. Too close.

"If I'd known you were in such a rush to leave, I could have kept you dry," he said, ignoring her snippy tone.

"Why would I tell you I was leaving? My plan was to leave you behind," Octavia huffed. "Obviously, I wasn't successful in that venture."

She wanted to slam her head against the wall. Why was Flynn following her? This forest was big enough for them both to travel through it without running into anyone. He had no reason to be so close to her, especially when he made her feel so many confusing things.

Flynn's handsome lips tilted down. "Why, Lady Octavia, you seem rather put out."

A laugh burst out of Octavia. She didn't attempt to hide her frustration as she balled her fists. "Now, *that's* an understatement. I was put out when I found you in my shack. That's no longer the case. Now, I'm angry. For the second time in one day, you've disrupted my plans."

Sure, those plans involved sleeping on the ground of this rocky cave and tossing and turning all night, but she was exhausted. Sleep sounded as good as a heap of gold to her right now. Since her hoards were far away and she couldn't shift, she'd take what she could get.

"You're angry... at me?"

Wow. Was he really that dense? Anger coursed through her, aimed at them both. Him, for obvious reasons, and herself, because she couldn't understand why she found this man attractive.

She wasn't an idiot—she was fairly certain he had ulterior motives, seeing as how he'd been searching through her bag earlier. He obviously wasn't just out for a leisurely stroll deep in the woods.

"Yes," she said curtly. Lifting her foot, she pulled her bag towards her. "You should leave."

Flynn stared down at her, his spine straightening. "Is that so?" He crossed his arms. "What if I don't want to leave? This cave isn't as nice as your shack, but it looks cozy."

Octavia's blood boiled. "I found it first." She was aware that she sounded slightly petulant, but she was done with this man. "I want you to go."

It was obvious by the way that Flynn looked at her that he didn't consider her a threat. She snarled, wishing she could shift. If she did, he wouldn't look at her like that anymore.

The dragon within Octavia uncoiled. Watching. Waiting.

They commanded us not to shift in possession of the object, the dragon reminded Octavia.

I know. Octavia stood and backed away from the witch. She couldn't go far, thanks to the tight quarters, but at least now he wasn't close enough to touch her. She absolutely did not want that.

You're angry, the dragon remarked unhelpfully.

Yes, Octavia snarled. *I am. This witch followed me. He deserves to know who he's dealing with.*

A pause. *If you break the council's rules, they will never accept us back. We will be forever banished. Is that what you want?*

Did Octavia want to be banished? Obviously not. She'd spent the past five decades trying to regain some semblance of a relationship with the other villagers.

But this witch just made her so *furious.* Especially because now, he tilted his head and watched her through those brown eyes that she'd remember for the rest of her life.

"I could leave," he murmured.

Octavia clutched her cane. "Then go."

He extended his palm, a solitary blue ribbon floating above his hand. "Or..."

The dragon shifter stared at the thread of magic. Damn that curiosity that had her repeating, "Or?"

He smirked. Gods, he did that a lot. "Or I could dry you off, and we could travel together."

Rationally, Octavia knew she shouldn't do it. She should insist he leave. But she was tired and hurting, and her feet were fucking wet. As she'd previously established, wet feet were the worst.

It was the squishiness between her toes that had her dipping her head. "Alright, you can stay... for now."

Flynn smiled and opened his palms. Ribbons swarmed from his hands. They flew around the dragon shifter before darting into her skin.

She gasped. Tingles spread all over her, warming her from the inside out. Steam rose from her clothes, and they dried in seconds. Dragon shifters naturally ran hot thanks to the fire in their veins—

some people called them furnaces—but even they couldn't make clothing miraculously dry.

"Thank you," Octavia forced out, hating that she had to be kind to this man who frustrated her so thoroughly. But she had manners, and she wouldn't let a kind act go unnoticed. She couldn't help but add, "You know, I'm still angry with you."

Flynn huffed a laugh. "I expected as much. You don't seem like one to easily let go of a grudge."

"I'm not."

He smiled as if this was nothing but a game. Then, without so much as a "by your leave," he slid down the other side of the cave and stretched his legs out in front of him. Placing his sword within arm's reach, he folded his arms in front of his chest and shut his eyes.

Octavia remained standing as she stared incredulously at the witch. "What are you doing?" she asked when it became clear he had no intention of moving.

Peeking open a single eye, Flynn's gaze crawled over the dragon shifter. "Sleeping. Or at least, I was trying to. You should do the same. The rain will stop tomorrow, and we'll have a long few weeks of hiking before we leave the forest."

"A few weeks?" she parroted. "No."

She couldn't imagine spending that much time with this man.

"Yes." His voice left no room for argument. "I like you, and traveling alone is rather tedious. We can part ways later when we get closer to our destinations."

Octavia narrowed her eyes. "What, exactly, is your destination?"

"Didn't I tell you?"

"No." She would've remembered. Frustratingly, she felt like she'd remember everything this witch told her.

A small smile. "I'm on my way to Vlarone."

"The city beneath the mountain?"

"The very one." His eyes slipped shut, and she knew this conversation was done for now.

That same curiosity flared within Octavia. She couldn't help it. Vlarone was the oldest city in the Rose Empire, built completely inside a mountain range. No one knew where it had come from. Some said it was gods-blessed. Others said giants had carved it out of the shale many years ago. Either way, it was supposedly beautiful —and far from Octavia's final destination.

She studied the witch for a long time. The dim light of the night didn't bother her, as she could see perfectly well, even in complete darkness. She wasn't sure what to do. Yes, she'd found Flynn digging through her bag, and he was definitely irritating, but he also hadn't harmed her. She didn't trust him for obvious reasons, but maybe traveling together for a bit wouldn't be so bad.

Kydona only knew that she could use the company.

What do you think? she asked her dragon. The creature was always rational, sometimes frustratingly so.

Flynn snored. How had he fallen asleep so quickly?

The dragon peeked out lazily, assessing the form of the man on the ground. *Stay with him for a few days, but don't trust him.*

Obviously. Octavia didn't trust anyone. Trust was just an opportunity to get hurt.

Sighing, Octavia shimmied to the ground. Propping up her ankle again, she crossed her arms. "Fine," she said. "I'll travel with you for a few days. But I reserve the right to leave at any time."

In response, the witch stopped snoring. He cracked open an eye and smiled. The twinkle in his gaze told her he'd already known she would agree.

"Good. You should sleep," he rumbled. "You look like you need it."

Octavia *was* tired. And cranky. And frustrated. A trifecta of unpleasantness.

Needless to say, with the handsome, irritating witch a few feet away from her, she did not find much rest that night.

THE SUN WAS SHINING when Octavia woke the following day after a night of restless sleep. Just like Flynn had predicted, the rain was gone. The air was lighter, and for the first time in a week, she could hear her thoughts instead of the constant rain.

Sunlight, actual gods-damned sunlight, shone into the cave. Dust particles danced in the rays as if celebrating the lack of rain.

It had only been a week, but it had felt like an entire lifetime had passed since Octavia had felt those warming rays. She eagerly rose, grabbed her walking stick, and hurried out of the cave. Relieving herself in some nearby bushes, she adjusted her tunic and leggings as she strolled back to the shelter.

It was only then that she realized the cave was empty.

A strange sensation burned in her chest, and she rubbed her fist over the pain.

Flynn had... left. Alright. That was fine. It wasn't like he owed the dragon shifter something. He must've woken this morning and reconsidered their travel arrangements. It wasn't like she had her heart set on them—after all, they'd just met yesterday when he was rifling through...

Her bag.

A million curses ran through Octavia's mind as she hobbled to the cave as quickly as possible. Her ankle was still sore, a sign that she'd overdone it yesterday. She found herself wishing for her brace. She'd stupidly left it in the shack when fleeing from Flynn. Evidently, that had been a mistake of epic proportions.

Thank Kydona, her satchel was exactly where she'd left it.

Octavia exhaled and dropped to her knees. Ignoring the cold stone pressing into her, she reached into the messenger bag until she felt the coolness she sought. Her fingers curled around the object, and she clutched the bag to her chest.

Never again. She'd keep her eyes on the bag every moment of every day from now until she made her delivery.

Several minutes passed until her breathing slowed.

Alone once again, Octavia gathered her thoughts and made a game plan for the day. She couldn't stay here, but with her ankle still sore, she'd have to be careful about how far she pushed herself.

First things first, food. Dragon shifters had voracious appetites, and Octavia wasn't an exception to that rule. Even though the thought of more trail rations made her grimace, she dug through her bag and pulled out a piece of dried meat. She was halfway through that unpleasant situation, the jerky lacking all flavor, when a twig cracked.

Octavia's head shot up as Flynn appeared at the front of the cave. His arms were full of apples, and he looked just as handsome as the day before.

"I thought you left," Octavia blurted.

The moment the words had left her mouth, she regretted them. Why was she like this? Why couldn't she smoothly interact with others? Instead, everything she said came out wrong.

The ghost of a smirk danced on Flynn's lips. "Miss me?" He didn't give her a chance to answer before he added, "I thought you might want a snack, but if you're not hungry..."

Cheeks flaming, Octavia shoved the half-finished piece of food into her bag. "It's really not delicious," she admitted. "I'd much prefer an apple... if you'll share."

A knowing smile danced across the witch's face. Gods help her, but her core twisted at the sight. "Of course. Here." He handed her one of the apples. The red flesh was soft but not bruised, and it smelled incredible.

What were the chances the apple was poisoned? Octavia considered it for a moment before tossing the thought aside. Flynn could've killed her ten times over by now if that was his goal.

Besides, it looked so good.

Perhaps a week ago, she would've spent more time thinking about this decision, but her stomach grumbled. With one final sniff, she took a big bite. Sweet, slightly tangy juices burst into her mouth, and she groaned. Spectacular. She'd never tasted something so delicious.

Octavia busied herself with inhaling the fruit, while Flynn

took a seat across from her.

Octavia ate as quickly as possible. When she was down to the seeds, the witch silently handed her another.

The dragon shifter devoured that one, too. After that, he gave her another one. She slowed, enjoying the flavors of the third apple.

When she finished, she looked up to find the witch staring at her. She took her time licking the sticky juices off her fingers. "What?"

Flynn shook his head, slowly eating an apple of his own. "You just... aren't what I expected."

Her eyes narrowed. They were doing that a lot around the witch. "What kind of expectations did you form in the twenty-four hours since you made my acquaintance?"

He lifted a shoulder. "I mean... I just don't know many ladies who eat like that."

This again? Octavia climbed to her feet, slung the messenger bag over her shoulder, and grabbed her walking stick. "Then it's a good thing I'm not a lady."

Flynn followed her out of the cave, smirking. Gods, why did that expression look so good on him? Every time she looked at him, it was like she discovered another way he was just perfectly handsome. Not pretty in a put-together way, but just... right.

Hearing her thoughts, Octavia mentally smacked herself. She needed to get it together. This would be a very long journey if her mind continued down this path.

The witch pointedly coughed. "As strangely delightful as it is to have you stare at me, perhaps we ought to get going? The more ground we cover through the day, the better."

"Just hiking, right?" Octavia confirmed. "That's it?"

He dipped his chin. "That's it."

Her eyes swept over him, searching for any sign of a lie. When she didn't see one, she nodded. "Fine. Lead the way."

Flynn was a talker.

Ten days had passed since their initial encounter in the small shack, and they were nearing the edge of the forest. They'd settled into a routine of sorts. They hiked during the day, stopping every few hours to get water from streams and eat whatever they could forage in the forests, and they would spend their nights in caves or under trees. They didn't light fires—it wasn't safe, even for a dragon shifter—but since the rain hadn't returned, the summer heat kept them warm enough.

They were as clean as they could get in the forest, washing up in streams and brooks, but Octavia missed the sensation of dunking her entire body underwater. When this was finished, she vowed to find a deep bathing pool and spend hours in it. She'd swim until her skin wrinkled. It would be amazing.

Through the hike, Octavia kept her bag on her at all times. Although she'd caught Flynn eyeing it on multiple occasions, he hadn't asked what was in it. Even if he did, she wouldn't tell him.

It was her secret.

As the days progressed, Flynn began talking Octavia's ear off. It wasn't that she didn't enjoy conversations—in the right circumstances, with the right topic, she could go for hours—but being an outcast for over five decades meant many of her social skills were out of practice.

"Did you know the merfolk throw a ball every year to celebrate the Summer Solstice?" Flynn asked, holding a branch aside so Octavia could duck under it.

She frowned. "No, and where did that thought come from?"

She'd quickly learned that Flynn's mind often jumped from one thing to the next, taking leaps that she sometimes had trouble following.

Moments ago, he'd been telling her about the various trees that made up the Rose Empire. She knew about them, having lived in the woods for most of her life, but redirecting the conversation would take more effort than necessary.

Flynn held out his hand and helped her over a twisted root.

"Summer Solstice is a week away."

Was it? Octavia paused, frowning. She hadn't realized that. Somewhere along the way, she must have lost track of time. Damn. The dragons in Firefall loved celebrating the Summer Solstice. A pang of disappointment went through Octavia when she realized she wouldn't be back in time. Few people in the Rose Empire threw celebrations like dragon shifters. Whether it was for a birth, a solstice, or a mating, dragon shifters loved to party.

Gods, that was just her luck. If the storm hadn't hit, she would've been able to return in time.

Despair twisted her stomach. Why did everything bad have to happen to her? Just when it seemed like things were turning around, something else would happen. What if she completed her delivery and returned to the village just in time for them to find another reason to ignore her? That would be horrible.

And yet...

For the first time, Octavia wondered why she cared so much. The villagers, who were supposed to be her family, had spent the better part of the past five decades ignoring her and making her feel horrible for her mistake. It had been an accident, but they constantly held it over her head. They'd been cruel to her, so why was it so important to her that they included her once again?

Even as she asked the question, Octavia knew the answer. Dragon shifters needed family. It was the same reason she craved touch. Kydona had created the shifters to live together in a unit.

Being alone meant she was missing an integral part of herself.

"Octavia?" Flynn took hold of her sleeve. "What's wrong?"

Her lips tilted down. "It's just—"

Her next words never came.

A pack of massive wolves, twice the size of normal ones, barrelled out of the woods. Snarling and yipping, they circled the pair.

Octavia's stomach dropped as she tightened her grip on her walking stick.

Flynn drew his sword. "Fuck."

CHAPTER 4
A Gods-Damned Cage

A witch and a dragon shifter with a bad ankle were no good against a pack of angry werewolves. Octavia knew instantly they were dealing with her shifter cousins. The orange eyes and larger-than-normal sizes were dead giveaways.

For the first time in nearly two weeks, common sense returned to Octavia. Thank all the gods for that. Swallowing, she dropped to her knees. Her walking stick fell beside her. Her right knee landed on a gnarled root, but she didn't dare move. She held up her hands in supplication. "We mean you no harm."

A chorus of snapping teeth and low growls was the only response.

Octavia inched her head around to look where Flynn still stood with his sword drawn. Did the witch have a death wish? It would be a real shame if his handsomeness were destroyed by the wolves. Especially since Octavia had come to... well, not enjoy, but tolerate his chatty presence enough that she didn't want to see him eaten by wolves.

Listen, her bar was fucking low.

Carefully moving so as not to anger the pack, Octavia tugged the leg of Flynn's trousers. "Get down," she hissed.

Octavia's heart thundered as the wolves inched closer. A long moment passed before Flynn sheathed his sword and dropped down beside the dragon shifter, his cloak fluttering.

The air seemed to breathe as the wolves circled the pair. Octavia didn't dare move, though her limbs quaked.

An all-black beast, a head taller than the others, pushed through the pack. His orange eyes landed first on Flynn, then Octavia.

The dragon shifter lifted her head, and though she trembled, she looked him in the eye. The black werewolf, obviously the leader, was a predator. But so was she. They didn't know she couldn't shift, and she intended to keep it that way.

The dragon peered out through Octavia's eyes, her attention curious but not on edge. *You've found yourself some werewolves,* she mused. *Interesting.*

Octavia stifled the growl rising within her. *It would be more interesting if they didn't look like they wanted to eat us.*

Perhaps if you'd been paying attention, you would've heard them.

Gods above, Octavia hated it when the dragon was right.

She was saved from having to reply when the black wolf snarled. The sound echoed through the forest, and the hairs on Octavia's neck rose. The other wolves yipped and pranced as a flash of white light burst from the wolf.

When it cleared, a tall shifter stood on two legs in front of them. He was naked. Very, very naked.

Octavia's eyes widened, and blood rushed to her cheeks. She saw... everything. How could she not? He was standing directly in front of her.

My goodness, the dragon purred.

Not happening, Octavia returned.

She dropped her gaze only to find Flynn's eyes on her. The weight of his stare caused her core to twist, and after a moment, she looked away.

"Who are you?" Octavia asked the werewolf, keeping her eyes on the ground.

A rumble ran through the wolves, likely because she dared to speak first, but it was the shifted man who growled, "You trespass on pack land and dare ask who *we* are?"

Octavia gulped, keeping her hands where they could see them. "I'm sorry, we didn't know." At the exact same time, Flynn said, "We were just traveling through."

Octavia's heart was a pounding hammer. The weight of the werewolf leader's stare was heavy, and she fought against the urge to bow her head to him. Reminding herself that she, too, was strong, she forced herself to breathe. To wait. To listen.

"The laws are clear," the leader replied harshly.

Fuck. Octavia's stomach dropped. Nothing good could come from the way the man glared at them or the violence that radiated from his aura.

The werewolf continued, "Trespassers on pack lands are subject to the Alpha's judgment. Take them."

Octavia cried out, and Flynn yelled as several flashes of white came from all around. The dragon shifter went to pull on her shift, Elders be damned, but before she could, something smashed into the back of her head.

Stars exploded in her vision, and then everything went black.

OCTAVIA'S BACK ACHED. Actually, scratch that. All of her hurt. This was worse than the time she'd tumbled out of the tree and hurt her ankle. Everything, from her head to her feet, throbbed painfully. Did she think the teeny-tiny shack was horrible?

This was far worse.

Then she opened her eyes. A curse Grandma Gertrude would have despised poured from Octavia's lips. She should've kept her eyes closed. Then she might've ignored this situation for a little while longer.

The dragon unfurled within Octavia. At least one good thing

had come from all this. It seemed like the creature was no longer ignoring her. *Where in the seven circles of hell are we?*

Octavia groaned. *Nowhere good, that's for certain.*

Iron bars surrounded her on all sides and rose above her head. The floor was cold and hard. Comfort didn't exist here.

Her stomach twisted in knots, her eyes widened, and bile rose in her throat.

She was in a gods-damned cage, like a fucking animal. Her bag was at her feet, but her walking stick was nowhere to be seen.

"Fucking hell," she cursed. How come these things kept happening to her?

A low, masculine grumble came from her left. "Quite the mouth on you, Lady Octavia."

She turned, her ankle protesting the movement. Flynn clutched the bars of his own cage, making no effort to hide his mirth.

"I'm sorry," Octavia snapped. "Is there something funny about this situation?"

There was little that Octavia hated more than being trapped. Dragons were meant to be free, to fly and soar through the skies. They weren't meant to be caged. Especially not next to too-handsome-for-their-own-good witches who apparently had horrible senses of humor.

Flynn had the audacity to smile. Smile!

As if being held captive by a pack of werewolves awaiting judgement from their Alpha was nothing but a joke to him.

It wasn't a joke to Octavia. This was one of the worst situations she'd ever found herself in, which said a lot.

"I find life is more enjoyable when you appreciate the small moments," Flynn said.

Octavia made a rude gesture at him. "Appreciate this."

He *laughed.*

Asshole.

Turning her back on the handsome, ridiculous witch, Octavia

curled up on the ground and drew her bag towards her. Pointedly ignoring Flynn, she took in their surroundings.

Long wooden beams stretched across the ceiling. Several windows filled with frosted glass let in the faint yellow glow of the sun, illuminating the dust swirling in the air. And the cages. There were a dozen of them in total, although the other enclosures were empty. Why did the werewolves have a dozen iron cages? Were there that many trespassers who threatened them?

A thought entered Octavia's mind, and she gasped. Maybe looking good wasn't the talkative witch's only use. Turning around, she clutched her bag to her chest and inched towards the bars.

Flynn watched her through amused brown eyes.

"Can you break us out of here?" she whispered. The thick bars were nearly the size of her hand. Even with her dragon shifter strength, she wouldn't be able to move them. But Flynn had magic.

"Maybe." His eyes sparked, and he held out his hand.

Seconds passed.

It seemed like something was supposed to happen, but there was nothing but empty air above his hand.

His brows furrowed, and a frown dug into his lips.

Strange. In the shack, his magic had seemed to come instantly. But maybe it would just take a little bit of time? She wasn't fully aware how his magic worked, so she would be patient.

Seconds became minutes.

Flynn's frown deepened, and his brows creased. "I can't reach my magic." For the first time since Octavia had met him, the witch seemed truly upset. "I can't... it's not there." His breath came faster and faster. "Where is it? Why can't I call on it?"

"Magic won't work," a small, soft voice said.

Octavia jolted, her gaze swiveling as she searched for the speaker.

A child, no more than ten, stood near their cages. The youngling's skin was a golden tan. She had long brown hair in two braids. Like the other werewolves they'd met, she had orange eyes. She wore a red frock and was barefoot, as though she'd been running through the woods.

"What do you mean?" Flynn asked. "What has been done to me?"

The panic was evident in his voice, and Octavia frowned. She might not have truly liked the witch, but she hated seeing anyone in pain.

"Magic doesn't work in the cages," the child said patiently. "They're lined with prohiberis."

Octavia knew of the magic-blocking metal. It was mined in the northern part of the Empire. Prohiberis was expensive and not easily located, but due to its ability to block everyone from their powers, including vampires and elves, it was highly sought after.

How did the werewolves have so much of it?

It was a pertinent question, but she would have to leave it for later because there was too much at hand right now.

"Gods damn it," Flynn swore.

The little girl gasped. "Oh, you said a bad word!" Her voice got louder, and she shook her head. "Daddy is going to be so mad at you. We don't say those kinds of words here."

A look of absolute indignation crossed Flynn's face, and Octavia stifled a giggle. Not so funny now, was he?

Luckily, Octavia knew how to talk with children. Often, they had been the only ones in Firefall who paid attention to her.

She crouched, keeping her bag in front of her, and smiled. "What's your name?" she asked, pressing her hand against the bars.

The child grinned at Octavia and walked towards her cage. "My name's Katiana, but most people call me Tia."

Tia's voice was soft and sweet, innocent even. Far different from the werewolves they'd encountered in the woods.

Octavia smiled. "It's a pleasure to make your acquaintance, Tia. My name is Octavia, and that grump over here is Flynn."

Tia waved, and a giggle slipped from her lips. Even Flynn cracked a smile at that. That was unsurprising. Who could stay angry when they were presented with such a display of cuteness? That was how children survived. They could be a lot, as Octavia had discovered many times when she looked after the village younglings, but every time she thought that she would never want to spend another moment with one of the little scoundrels, they smiled or did something sweet, and that she was right back to where she'd been before.

One day, she hoped to have her own.

"Why are you in the cages kept for the wolves who can't control their shift?" Tia asked.

Tucking that nugget of knowledge away for later, Octavia sighed, "Flynn and I don't know. We woke up here."

"Oh." The youngling frowned. "That's not good."

No, it definitely wasn't.

"It's my fault," Flynn said, sounding contrite. That was new, and Octavia wasn't sure how she felt about that. "I hadn't realized we crossed into your pack lands."

Tia frowned and studied the two of them. "So, this was a mistake."

"Yes, an unfortunate one." Flynn caught Octavia's gaze and held it. His voice lowered, and a deep emotion flickered in his eyes. "Lady Octavia didn't know where we were. I led us here."

Octavia's brows furrowed. There was a softness in Flynn's voice that she hadn't heard before. Something within her twisted. She wasn't immune to apologies, and right now, it sounded like Flynn was trying to do exactly that.

"A lady!" Tia gasped. "Oh, my gods. I've never met a lady before." The child did a funny hop-dance as she darted away from the cage. "I'm going to tell Daddy he must be nice to you. A lady!"

Before Octavia could correct the child for her mistake, Tia was running away. The door opened, giving a momentary glimpse of brilliant, unmuted sunshine before it banged shut.

They were alone agone.

Octavia turned back to the witch. "Why do you keep calling me that? I told you, I'm not a lady."

There weren't many lords and ladies in the Rose Empire who ventured away from the capitol. Octavia had never met one before. It was rare for the upper classes to lower themselves enough to visit the dragon shifters' isolated villages.

A lazy grin swept over Flynn's face. His discomfort of not having his magic seemed to be far away now. "Maybe I just like the way your eyes light up when I call you that."

A growl rumbled through Octavia. "I'm finding the more time we spend together, the less I like you."

The witch with the obnoxious good looks rocked back on his heels. "Do you want to know what I think?"

"Nope, but I bet you're going to tell me anyway." He was irritating like that. In fact, Octavia had never met anyone who irritated her more than Flynn.

"I think you just don't want to admit you like me."

See? She was right. He just couldn't seem to stop trying to get a rise out of her. Well, good for him. He succeeded. Octavia gasped and crossed her arms. "I do not!"

An infuriating smirk ghosted Flynn's lips. "Really? Can you truthfully tell me you haven't been thinking about what it would be like between us?" He leaned closer, reaching an arm between their cages. His fingers grazed the edge of hers. "Because you've been haunting my dreams, Octavia. Every night, as I sleep, I see the two of us together. Your spark, your fire intrigues me."

Octavia was speechless, which didn't happen often. Her mouth fell open, and she stared at the witch. Sure, Flynn had made a few such comments while they hiked, but she'd brushed them aside. She hadn't thought he was serious.

But right now, with that look on his face, he looked serious. In fact, this was the most serious she had seen him. "I've wanted you since that first day in your cabin," he admitted. "And I think you want me too."

Was the dragon shifter speechless before? That was nothing compared to her current inability to speak.

Her cheeks burned. She didn't want to lie. Obviously, she

thought Flynn was insanely attractive, and he'd starred in more than a few of her dreams since they met, but she wasn't sure if she was ready to tell him that. It felt... serious, and a part of her knew that admitting those things would be something that she could not take back.

It was one thing to find Flynn both incredibly handsome and vexing, but it would be another entirely to admit her feelings. Luckily, Octavia was saved from having to answer when the doors banged open once again.

The werewolf from the forest entered, though he was clothed now. His brown hair had been pulled back into a long ponytail, and he wore a black tunic. Standing next to him was a burly, muscular man whose aura screamed, *leader*. His chestnut hair was shoulder-length, black ink wrapped around his neck like a choker, and two swords were crossed behind his back. His skin was tanned and dark, as though he'd spent hours and hours in the sun.

This was the Alpha. There was no doubt about it.

The pair came to a stop in front of the cages. The Alpha crossed his arms, and his orange eyes glinted shrewdly as his gaze slowly moved from Flynn to Octavia. "You trespassed on our lands."

The way he said it, one would think they had killed his prized puppy and not missed a land marker.

Tension rose and rose, and Octavia's skin crawled. Something about the two men standing in front of her told her they would be lucky if they left these cages alive.

Octavia gulped, meeting the Alpha's gaze. "We didn't mean to. It was an accident."

The Alpha ignored her. "Do you know what we do with trespassers?"

"You set them free with a warning?" Octavia asked hopefully, wondering if maybe, just this once, things could go her way.

"No," the leader snarled, slamming his hand on the bars of the dragon shifter's cage.

The iron rattled, and pain shot through Octavia's ankle. She squeaked, scrambling away from the werewolf. Octavia wasn't proud of her reaction, but what else was she supposed to do? She was weaponless, without even her walking stick.

Shifting was strictly prohibited, although she would do it if it saved her life. But she wasn't sure what would happen if she shifted in an iron cage lined with prohiberis—would it break, or would she?

"My sincerest apologies." Flynn pressed his hand over his heart, drawing the Alpha's attention to him. "I was escorting the lady, and somehow, I missed your pack land markers. We did not intend to trespass, and we will happily leave immediately."

"You may not have meant to come here, but you did," the Alpha barked, his eyes flashing. "You—"

"Daddy!" A high-pitched squeal filled the space as Tia barreled in and slammed into the Alpha's legs.

The man growled, "Katiana, what are you doing here? You're supposed to be with Nyshali right now. Daddy is busy."

"Nyshali is at the river," Tia said. "I was too, but then I left."

The Alpha sighed, the sound long-suffering. "Why?"

"To find you!" Tia jumped into her father's arms, ignoring the others in the room.

Scowling, the Alpha glared at his daughter before hoisting her up and setting her snuggly on his hip.

Octavia stared at the werewolf. With a small child attached to him, the leader looked far more approachable than he had before. Maybe they would survive this. Doubtful, but maybe.

"This isn't a good time, Katiana," the Alpha admonished as he stepped away from the cages. "I need to deal with the prisoners. Go find Nyshali and tell her she's to meet me in an hour to discuss her... abilities to watch you."

"What? No! You can't hurt them, Daddy!" Katiana's eyes widened, and she clutched her father's tunic. "Please tell me you won't hurt them."

Octavia wasn't sure how she had earned such a fervent protectress, but she would happily take Tia's help. She'd accept anyone's help right now. This had *not* been a good month. Between the endless rainstorm, Flynn breaking into her cabin, and now being held prisoner, Octavia was ready to write off this entire year as horrible.

The Alpha sighed and tried to put his daughter down. "You know it's my job. I have to protect the pack, and sometimes that means—"

"No!" Tia screeched and slammed her arms against her father's chest, railing against him. "You can't! She's a *lady*,"—she emphasized the last word like it mattered—"and I like her."

Hope sparked deep within Octavia.

"Pumpkin, this is a matter for grownups."

And just like that, the Alpha squashed all her hopes.

Tia's lip wobbled, and tears lined her eyes. "But Daddy, she seems really nice."

Everyone's eyes, including Flynn's, swung to Octavia. Recognizing the importance of her response in the next few moments, Octavia forced a smile on her face. At least, she attempted to smile. It was difficult, considering the current situation.

"My name is Octavia Ashbloom." She kept her head low and her voice quiet. "I swear to you, I'm harmless."

Except when you shift and lose control of your fire, the dragon unhelpfully added.

Octavia shushed her. This was not the time for those types of comments.

"What's in the bag?" the werewolf from the woods asked Octavia warily.

Out of habit, she pulled the bag towards her. "Nothing, really. Food, a water bottle, a change of clothes, and a few miscellaneous items."

Including the very important one that she'd vowed to deliver unharmed.

Keeping the smile plastered on her face, Octavia willed herself to appear as unimposing as possible. It wasn't exactly easy since dragon shifters naturally gave off predatory auras, but she did her best. "I swear on Kydona herself, we mean you no harm."

At this point, Octavia would say just about anything to get out of this alive. She wasn't the most religious of all dragons, but that might change if she survived this.

The werewolves' glares were filled with the promise of power and simmering violence. Although Octavia wanted to look away, she didn't dare.

"What do you think, Bren?" the Alpha asked the other wolf.

His eyes narrowed. "It's up to you, sir. I don't like the look of them."

That didn't sound good. Octavia tried to make herself smaller as the Alpha kept staring at her.

"Please, Daddy." Tia wrapped her arms around the Alpha's neck and squeezed. "Will you spare them? For me?"

Octavia's heart hammered. Every breath felt too loud as she waited and waited.

A monumental sigh that sounded like it could shake mountains escaped the Alpha. His lips pursed, and then he groaned. "Fine," he said, although it sounded like it wasn't. "I'll spare their lives, but they can't stay here. Trespassing is not acceptable behavior, and we don't condone it."

Octavia had gleaned that much from the cages.

"Can they have dinner with us before they leave?" Tia added hopefully.

Another sigh. Octavia got the distinct impression that the Alpha had his hands full with his daughter.

"Pleaseeeeeee," Tia begged. "Let them stay one night. It's already late afternoon, and you should feed them. It's the right thing to do."

As if on cue, Octavia's stomach grumbled. She hadn't yet considered how long they'd been in the cages, but judging by the emptiness in her stomach, it had been quite some time.

"Fine. They can come *if* they're guarded." The werewolf glared at the pair of prisoners. "You wouldn't be stupid enough to try anything, right?"

Octavia shook her head, and Flynn said, "No, sir."

So, it turned out the witch was in possession of some manners, after all.

"Okay." The Alpha nodded. "Release them, Bren, and fit them with cuffs. I won't have any stray magic near the pack. We'll put them up for the night, and they can leave first thing in the morning."

"Thank you, Daddy!" Their little savior pressed a series of slobbery kisses on her father's cheeks as he turned and strode away. Tia waved from over her father's shoulder, and Octavia smiled weakly back.

Then Bren opened the lock, and his hand reached inside the cage. "Come here."

CHAPTER 5
Dinner with a Side of Awkward Conversations

The cage was bad, but the prohiberis cuffs were horrible. Bren hadn't been kind when he put them on Octavia's wrists, but she hadn't complained. Her discomfort seemed so small compared to Flynn's. The witch had started sweating profusely the moment the cuffs had been slapped onto him. His face was ashen, and he grunted in pain as he walked next to Octavia.

Flynn's sword and her walking stick were still nowhere to be seen.

The village Bren led them through reminded Octavia of Firefall. Longhouses stood tall, flourishing gardens surrounded them, and the wind carried children's laughter to their ears. Twilight cast shadows upon them as they walked, and people stared at them, but Octavia didn't look back. The prohiberis cuffs were heavy, and her foot had a heartbeat of its own. Her bag hung over her shoulder, hitting her hip rhythmically.

Bren led them into the furthest longhouse. Two large werewolves sat across a roaring fire, their gazes dark as they stared menacingly at them.

"Take a seat." Bren gestured to the empty log. "Your dinner will be here soon." Then, as if the men staring them down from across the fire weren't sending enough of a message, Bren added, "Don't try anything."

As if. This was obviously someone's home, with blanket-covered pallets lining the walls. It seemed homey, although there was no one else there.

Deciding the best thing she could do was obey, Octavia dropped onto the empty log. Flynn sat next to her. It was nice to be out of the cage, and her body appreciated the lack of bars around them. She stretched out her legs and wiggled her toes.

Silence filled the longhouse, the crackling of logs the only sound.

The cuffs grew heavier and heavier. Unbidden, Octavia's mind filled with memories of Firefall. The snapping of burning wood, the crisp scent of smoke, and the deep, comforting smell of burning wood reminded her of home.

A few minutes later, a woman wearing a black dress and a white apron entered with four plates. She was silent, handing them first to the men across the fire, then to Octavia and Flynn.

"Thank you," Octavia said.

The quiet woman smiled and dipped her head.

"Ylana," one of the men growled. "Go."

Her smile dropped, and she hurried out of the longhouse.

When Ylana was gone, Octavia's gaze dropped to the plate in her lap. A quarter roasted chicken, some sort of mash, and leafy greens looked and smelled heavenly. It had been too long since she had a proper meal.

Still, she was cognizant that the werewolves weren't pleased with their presence here. She waited until the men across the fire took their first bites before she dug in.

The moment the roasted meat hit her tongue, she moaned. Good gods, she was starving. She devoured the entire plate, eating every single morsel before running her finger through the fat and licking that off. She felt full for the first time in over a month.

By the time her plate was empty, the guards were no longer intently staring at them. They seemed to realize she and Flynn weren't an immediate threat and they'd returned to conversing quietly together.

"Wasn't that delicious?" Octavia smacked her lips. "I think roasted chicken..."

Her words trailed off as she glanced at Flynn for the first time since getting her food.

Oh, gods.

He looked... well, terrible. For Flynn. For a regular person, he was still insanely attractive. But for him? Pain was etched on his countenance, and his plate was still full.

Her gaze dropped to his hands, and she gulped. Flaming skin sat beneath his manacles.

She gasped, reaching out to touch him before pulling back. "Flynn, your hands. Are they hurting?"

Internally, she berated herself for asking such a stupid question. Of course, they were hurting. Blisters were breaking out on his skin.

He grimaced. "A bit," was his evasive answer. "I'll be fine."

She'd seen birds with broken wings that looked more fine than him. But she could tell he didn't want her to pry.

"Alright," Octavia sighed. She wouldn't push if he didn't want her to.

Though their longhouse was quiet, others were nearby. If she focused, she could hear the hushed conversations. It wasn't eavesdropping as much as... paying attention to her surroundings.

"Did you hear about the merfolk? They..."

"The Spirits of the Woods are..."

"... Thelrena herself would never trust her Earth Elves to..."

And below those normal conversations were whispers that normal human ears wouldn't be able to hear. But Octavia wasn't a lady, nor was she human, and her hearing was far from normal.

"Did you see them?" someone asked.

She imagined that furtive glances were shot in the direction of the longhouse.

"I heard they were..."

And even quieter, "The handsome one is a witch. That's why the Alpha insisted they wear the prohiberis."

A tittering laugh. "He's a looker, isn't he? If I weren't mated to Tor, I would take him back to my longhouse and..."

Octavia turned her head, her cheeks flaming as she rubbed her temples. She didn't need to overhear some random werewolf's plans about Flynn. She wasn't his keeper, and he could do whatever he wanted... even if the thought made her stomach twist.

Octavia told herself that her discomfort had everything to do with the prohiberis cuffs on her wrist and nothing to do with jealousy. She had no claim on Flynn. He could do whatever he wanted with whomever he wanted. They were both adults and fully capable of making their own decisions.

That's what she told herself.

The dragon wanted the witch. *Octavia* wanted the witch. She'd tried to ignore it, but it was becoming an inevitable truth. She didn't like him much, but she was drawn to him. It was becoming more difficult each day to remember why she wasn't acting on her desire.

She could think of several reasons why they should be together.

First, they were both Mature. Not only that, but Flynn was incredibly attractive. While Octavia would never claim to be the most beautiful dragon in Firefall, she certainly wasn't ugly. Additionally, she didn't have a husband or mate to speak of.

But maybe...

Oh gods. Did Flynn already have a partner? Octavia would never involve herself with another woman's man. She didn't do things like that.

Suddenly, finding out if Flynn had a witch back home became the most important thing on the dragon shifter's mind. Octavia turned, intent on asking Flynn if he had a partner when her nostrils flared.

Copper filled the air.

All thoughts of kissing and other more pleasant activities

vanished from her mind. She gasped, "Oh, my gods! Flynn, you're bleeding."

Crimson dripped from his wounds onto the dirt below their feet.

Flynn slowly looked over at Octavia, his face as pale as snow.

"Am I?" He sounded dazed, and he wobbled on the log. "How odd. I hadn't even noticed."

How could he have not noticed? Blood was pooling beneath them.

She stood, her plate tumbling to the ground.

Instantly, the two guards growled at her. Octavia refused to let them intimidate her.

"He's hurt!" she exclaimed, pointing to Flynn.

"So?" The bigger of the two guards raised a brow and shrugged. "Why should we care?"

Ass. "Because he's bleeding!"

It was one thing for Octavia to be annoyed by Flynn. It was another thing entirely for these werewolves to disrespect him.

Their behaviour rankled Octavia, although she wasn't sure exactly why.

A wolfish snarl was the only reply from across the fire.

Fury was a living fire within Octavia. It grew by the second, kindled by the dispassioned way the guards looked at her.

"He needs help." Obviously.

"Does he?"

"Yes," she growled.

Her heart pounded. Her lungs squeezed.

Fingers grazed hers, the touch gentle and sending sparks through her. "Octavia, it's alright. It's just the prohiberis," Flynn whispered. "It affects me differently, that's all."

It absolutely was not alright. It was one thing to hold them prisoner, but the Alpha had already spared their life. This punishment was cruel.

"Help him, please," Octavia asked the guards.

This time, they didn't even bother to reply. Ignoring her

completely, they turned to each other to continue their prior conversation.

Anger bubbled within Octavia. Red tinged her vision. Deep within, the dragon woke.

Dueling desires warred within her. She was a fucking alpha in her own right. A dragon. These werewolves wouldn't ignore her if they knew what she was. Their nonchalance made Octavia so... so...

"Octavia." A firm hand gripped her shoulder, spinning her around so her back was to the fire. The Alpha stood behind her. "You need to calm down."

"I am calm," she growled.

Her blood heated in her veins, betraying her lie even as smoke filled the back of her mouth. Apparently, dragons could still pull on the shift even with prohiberis because she could feel the instinctual need rising within her.

The Alpha's eyes widened, and a flash of recognition went through them. He grabbed Octavia's arm and yanked up her sleeve, exposing her flesh. Purple scales crawled over her skin.

The Alpha's orange eyes flashed with fire, and pure command laced his words as he ordered, "Calm. The. Fuck. Down."

Octavia's heart was a war drum in her chest, bringing her closer and closer to the raging inferno threatening to burst out of her.

How dare the werewolf try to command her? He didn't have the right to tell her what to do. He wasn't her alpha. She wasn't one of his wolves that he could order around.

Anger was burning lava roiling through Octavia.

She needed...

She needed...

What did she need? A red fog took over her mind, clouding everything from sight. Her brain was hot. Too hot.

The dragon sat on its haunches. Watching. Waiting. A predator biding her time before she pounced.

Octavia's leash on her control slipped, and her lips curled into a sneer. Suddenly, shifting was the only thing on her mind. She would release her dragon, expand her wings, and roar so vociferously that none of them would know what hit them.

They'd think twice before refusing to treat... to treat...

Her brows knit together. Thinking was far too difficult as the animal took over. Why was she so upset? She knew there was a reason she probably shouldn't do this, but no matter how hard she tried, she couldn't remember what it was.

Someone touched her hand.

A snarl rose within Octavia, but it died off when a pair of familiar brown eyes moved in front of her.

She liked those eyes. They made her feel... safe.

Why was that? For the life of her, she couldn't figure it out.

"Hey beautiful, look at me," Flynn breathed. "I'm fine. See?"

Did she see that? She wasn't sure he was fine. Sweat shone on his forehead, and he was incredibly pale. But there was something about his face that made her calm down. Her heart rate slowed, her breathing leveled out, and the red cleared.

Bit by bit, minute by minute, the dragon returned to its slumber.

When Octavia's mind was her own once more, her gaze swept over the witch. "Flynn, are you okay?"

He nodded slowly. Octavia reached out to touch him, but before she could, a hand snatched hers.

"Dinner is *over*," the Alpha declared, twisting Octavia's wrist. His grip was just on this side of pain. "You two will leave first thing tomorrow, as promised. Tonight, we'll put you up in a... guest house." He frowned. "A heavily guarded one. This way."

Without waiting for a response, the Alpha turned. He clearly expected them to follow.

Octavia stared at the werewolf, confusion twisting deep within. The dinner she'd eaten was like lead in her stomach. She'd never been so close to letting her leash on the dragon slip before.

What was happening to her?

"This can't be right." Octavia crossed her arms and glared at the werewolf standing just inside the doorway of the so-called guest quarters.

The white-washed cabin was small, nothing like the longhouse where they'd just been, and though it was dark, she could make out the prohiberis lining the walls. That must be the reason the tall, blond guard had removed the cuffs when they stepped inside. Violence radiated from him, and he didn't look like he had a kind bone in his body.

The werewolf snarled, baring elongated canines in her direction. "I assure you, this is where the Alpha wants you to stay."

Octavia looked around the cabin and sputtered, "But... but there's only one bed!"

And it wasn't one of those kingly beds she imagined one would find in the Emerald Palace. No, this was more of a cot than a bed, and it looked uncomfortable at best. It definitely wasn't built for two people. The entire cabin was maybe twice the size of the shack they'd left in the woods.

A smirk crawled across the smug werewolf's mouth, making the dragon shifter want to introduce her fist to his face. "My goodness, you're an observant one, aren't you?"

Octavia growled. "You little—"

"Enough, Octavia." Flynn pulled her behind him. He pushed her towards the back wall and put himself between the two snarling predators. "This will be just fine. Thank you."

The guard grunted something resembling a farewell, in the loosest sense of the term, and drew the door shut. At the last minute, he added, "Don't try anything. You'll be under heavy guard until it's time to leave."

Because of her. Flynn might have gotten them into this mess, but there was no denying that Octavia had caused a few problems at dinner.

Her cheeks flammed, and she studied the ground. Her behavior was not acceptable, especially not a Mature shifter who was trying to regain the Elders' favor.

Groaning, Octavia tossed her bag in the corner of the room, as far from the door as she could get it. The only good thing about this change of scenery was that they'd removed the cuffs. "Let me see your hands."

Flynn sucked in a breath, but he slowly extended his wrists towards her. She didn't need the moonlight shining through the solitary window to see the ruby tint to his skin or the tiny welts that marked the place where the cuffs had been.

Her fingers traced his skin, and his breath hitched. "I'll be fine," Flynn said gruffly. "Once we leave, I can heal myself."

Octavia frowned. "You shouldn't have to wait. Maybe I could convince the guard to let you walk around away from the prohiberis. Then you could—"

"No." He stepped towards her. "It's fine."

The witch kept using that word, but Octavia didn't think he understood what it meant.

"Flynn—"

"Octavia." Her name was little more than a growl as it slipped from his mouth. "It's *fine*."

And this time, she understood what he was trying to say.

She looked up at him, and their eyes locked. His gaze smoldered, and he looked at her like she was the only person in the whole world.

Flynn took another step closer. There was barely any room between them.

Suddenly, Octavia became aware of just how small this space was. A bed, a chair, and a slim wardrobe took up most of the room. A jug of water sat on the only nightstand. That was it. The guard had told them there was an outhouse outside, but she didn't want to have to deal with the nasty werewolf or have more prohiberis put on her. She'd just... hold it. Still, even though this wasn't high-class living, it was a hundred times better than the cages.

And Flynn...

Octavia realized she was still gripping his wrists. Still staring at him. Still standing just a few inches from him.

But instead of moving away, she studied him. She couldn't help it—she drank him in. Every single part of him intrigued her in a way that nothing else ever had.

Stubble grew from their days in the forest, the hints of a red beard a few shades lighter than his hair. His chest was smooth and hard. He was muscular, unlike her. She'd always enjoyed food, and dragon shifters had voracious appetites. Her body was proof of that, and she was proud of it.

Flynn breathed her name, the word a hoarse whisper on his lips.

Octavia's core twisted, and she squeezed her thighs together as desire pulsed through her. Who knew one word could have such an effect on a person?

She dragged her gaze up to his. "Yes?"

"You can let go of my wrists now, beautiful."

Twice now, he'd called her that. She could say it didn't affect her, but she'd be lying.

She released his wrists but didn't move. She couldn't. Her heart was a thundering horse, and her lungs were tight. She felt like a youngling preparing for their first shift. Unprepared and excited for the unknown, all at once.

Octavia recalled her question from earlier. "Do you... at home..." The words weren't coming easily. Inhaling deeply, she took a readying breath and then plowed ahead. "What I'm asking is whether you have someone at home. A witch or an elf or... whatever? It's great if you do, and if that's the case, I'll just go away, but maybe—"

He put his finger on her lips, silencing her rambling. "No."

He closed the gap between them. Her breasts brushed against his chest, and she forgot how to breathe.

Then, his words settled upon her.

No. He had someone. Her shoulders dropped, and stupid tears

rushed to her eyes. Of course, Flynn was taken. Why would a handsome, young witch not have a partner?

"Oh, okay." Octavia blinked furiously, hoping that witches didn't have extraordinary vision like dragons. She didn't need him to know tears were threatening to fall. "Sorry. I'm just going to... go."

She turned, but there was no escape. They were trapped here until the morning.

Why hadn't she thought about that before? She'd stepped out of her comfort zone and failed horribly.

There were probably several more decades of celibacy in her future. So much for children. After this, Octavia would likely never talk to another man again. Maybe she'd join one of those convents dedicated to honoring the goddesses. She would—

Warm breath danced across her ear, and she stiffened.

"I don't have a girlfriend at home," Flynn murmured.

"Boyfriend, then?" She didn't turn around. It was far too easy to picture Flynn with another man. Was he also a witch? Did they do spells together?

"No." His hand found her arm and squeezed. "Octavia, I have no one."

A note of loneliness entered his voice, but as soon as it was there, it disappeared.

"No one?" Octavia slowly turned around.

"None." He was still touching her. "How about you? Is there someone lucky?"

She snorted. "Nope." No one wanted to be with the village outcast. "Not at all."

She was hopelessly, forever alone. Destined for a life without anyone else. Was she being dramatic?

Maybe.

But it was the truth.

She would—

Flynn's lips crashed into hers.

CHAPTER 6

I Thought This Would Help

For one singular moment, Octavia didn't react. She just stood there, putting all her weight on her good leg, as Flynn kissed her.

And gods above, what a kiss it was.

His mouth moved over hers with the practiced skill of someone who'd done this many times over. This wasn't just a kiss —it was as though he'd been holding back from the moment they met. Sparks ran through Octavia, starting at her mouth and making their way through her.

And then his tongue touched the seam of her lips. It sent a jolt through her, just like his magic had back in the shack. Whatever strange restraint had frozen her in place snapped like a too-tight lyre string.

Octavia moaned. Her right hand found Flynn's hip, and her left wove behind his neck as she held him close. Before she could think too hard about the consequences of her actions—she was fairly certain this wasn't an exceedingly wise decision—she kissed him back.

Their mouths slanted together. Lips and tongues and teeth competed for attention as they kissed and kissed and kissed.

Flynn's tongue swept into Octavia's mouth, and he tasted her like she was the most exquisite food.

"Good gods, Octavia," he groaned against her lips. Each word was punctuated by a nip to her mouth, her chin, her neck. Each second brought her closer to completely melting against him. "I thought this would help."

His fingers threaded behind her neck, and he held her close. He kissed her like she was air and he was drowning. Like she was the answer to all his life's problems, and he'd just found her. He kissed her in a way that didn't make sense.

How could they feel this way after knowing each other for such a short time?

"Help what?" she gasped, unable to fully draw breath beneath the weight of his attention. Not that she really cared. Who needed to breathe when they were being kissed like this?

"Don't you feel it?" He squeezed her hip, his hands apparently no longer bothering him. "The pull between us?"

Octavia sucked in a breath, and her heart hammered. "I thought it was just me."

Or at least, mostly on her side of things. Despite the things he'd said, she'd dismissed his words as playful banter. Why would the handsome witch be interested in her? She was just an injured messenger who couldn't even shift right now.

Flynn laced their fingers together. His forehead pressed against hers, and his breath was coming as unevenly as hers.

"Just you?" He let out a grim chuckle and guided her hand between them to the obvious bulge in his trousers. "Does this feel like I'm unaffected by you, Lady Octavia?"

Objections to his calling her a lady again rose to her tongue, but then he pressed her hand against his cock. Oh gods. It wasn't like Octavia was a virgin, but fifty years with just a few drunken trysts didn't exactly chalk up to a lot of experience.

And this was... he was... thick.

"I... oh," she said.

What else could she say?

He growled her name and added, "You're beautiful."

"Me?" Octavia blinked up at the witch. "You're the one who's beautiful."

There was no doubt in her mind that he was goddess-blessed.

The hand that was laced through hers lifted, cupping her cheek instead. The red marks from the prohiberis were still there, but he was no longer bleeding, and Octavia was inclined to believe the witch when he said they didn't hurt.

"When you say things like that, Octavia, it makes it very hard to..." His brows knit together, and for a moment, it seemed like he was going to say something else. Silence stretched between them before he shook his head. "All the werewolves were watching you tonight."

She tilted her head. "Yes, because we're their prisoners."

She hadn't forgotten that crucial fact. This guesthouse was a step up from the cages, but it was still a prison.

Flynn shook his head. "No. Because you draw everyone's attention like a moth to a flame."

Octavia's mouth fell open. She didn't have a chance to say anything because Flynn bent, kissing her again. His lips were still locked on hers as he nudged her towards the bed. Not that it was difficult—the room boasted little else.

The back of her legs hit the mattress, and she gasped, "Flynn, wait."

Instantly, he broke away. She could still feel everything through the thin barrier of their clothes. Her chest heaved in time with his. Her heart pounded, and though faint tinges of pain ran from her ankle up through her leg, it didn't hurt nearly as bad as it should have.

"Yes?" His eyes searched hers. "What do you want, Octavia?"

The question brought her pause. On one hand, she wanted him. She'd felt that way since the moment they met. On the other hand, she hadn't forgotten the way they'd met. She'd found him rummaging through her bag.

Octavia might've found Flynn extremely attractive, but she wasn't a complete idiot. Red flags abounded around him.

"I want you," she admitted. The witch growled, but she put her left hand on his chest. "I'm just worried this is moving a little fast."

Even having acknowledged that this was probably a bad decision, Octavia was moments away from letting Flynn ravage her. What did that say about the dragon shifter? She wasn't sure if she was ready to unpack that.

Flynn hitched a breath. "What if we took sex off the table?"

Octavia's brows jumped to her hairline. That was rather presumptive of him. "Who says it's on the table?"

His gaze dropped pointedly to her right hand, which was still feeling him intimately.

Blood rushed to Octavia's cheeks, and she yanked back her arm. "Oh, my gods. I just... you were... it's very nice," she finished lamely.

Was there a hole nearby? Octavia wanted to crawl into it and never, ever, ever come out again. There would never be a more perfect moment for the sky to fall.

A booming chuckle burst from Flynn's chest and filled the small room. "Thank you."

Octavia's chest burned, and drawing breath was nearly impossible. She was fairly certain she'd never been so embarrassed in her entire life. How had she not realized she was feeling him up?

The dragon shifter moved, hoping to turn around, but in her haste, she forgot about the bed behind her. Octavia's foot caught on the edge of the navy bedspread. Instead of moving away like she'd intended, she twisted her foot. Her bad one.

"Ow!" she cried out. Losing her balance, she slammed all her weight down on her bad leg. A mangled groan escaped her, and she cursed. Unsurprisingly, the foul language didn't ease the pain.

"Shit." Flynn reached for her. "What's wrong? Is it your foot?"

"Yes," Octavia forced the word through her clenched jaw and pointed at the offending appendage.

Flynn's brows creased. "Can I take a look?"

"It's a very old injury," she said. She was certain he'd noticed it before. It wasn't like she hid her limp or her walking stick.

"Still, I'd like to see. If you'll allow me."

His tone was so sincere that Octavia found herself nodding. Moments later, Flynn's arms swept under her. He gingerly placed her in the middle of the bed as though she were made of glass. His skilled fingers drew up her legging with care. She propped herself up on her elbows and watched as his deft fingers ran over her ankle.

He touched a particularly sore spot, and she hissed.

"Sorry," he muttered.

His touch was even lighter after that as he rolled down her sock. Everywhere he touched, jolts of awareness ran through her.

"How does it look?" Octavia asked although she didn't really want to know.

He frowned, and gods help her if he looked handsome even now. "You turned your ankle." He ran his index finger over the injury. "But it wasn't the first time."

Octavia's throat thickened as memories of falling out of the tree flashed through her mind. The forests around Firefall were massive, and her mother had always warned her away from climbing the tallest trees. Octavia hadn't listened, and this was her constant reminder. "I had an accident many years ago. Suffice it to say, trees and I are no longer on friendly terms." She shrugged, trying to play it off, but she didn't think she was successful.

Flynn frowned, still running his fingers over her ankle. "I noticed your limp, but I thought... I didn't realize how bad it was. I'm sorry."

Octavia's breath caught in her throat. Usually, when people noticed the mangled skin around her ankle and the slightly disjointed bone, they stared. Sometimes, they made rude comments—both within her earshot and out of it. Other times, their conversation became stilted and awkward when they realized she'd been hurt in the past.

No one had ever just acknowledged how incredibly... crappy the situation was.

Gods, this was making Octavia feel things she had no business feeling after knowing the witch for only two weeks.

Her gaze rose and met his, locking once again. This time, it was like her entire world stopped. Her heart ceased pounding. Her lungs seized. Fire coursed through her. Her core coiled. Entire lifespans passed as they stared at each other.

Flynn *saw* her. He really, truly saw her.

And she felt... everything.

She whispered his name and held his gaze. Her heart pounded, its rhythm echoing in her ears. *Bad idea, bad idea, bad idea.*

Except... she couldn't seem to remember why this was a bad idea. All she remembered was that Flynn looked at her like she mattered, and that was more important than anything else.

The beat of her heart shifted. *He sees you. He cares.*

Flynn hadn't hurt her in spite of the strange circumstances of their meeting and the forcefulness with which she'd tried to push him away. Maybe it would be okay to just... be with him. For a little while. What was the worst thing that could happen?

Throwing caution to the wayside, Octavia swallowed. "Will you hold me?"

Her voice was soft, and she was almost afraid to hear the answer. It had been so long since anyone had just... been with her.

"Of course." The mattress dipped beneath Flynn's weight as he stretched out alongside her. He was bigger than her in all the ways that mattered, and yet, he fit beside her perfectly.

Her heart pounded at his nearness.

His arm swept over her, and he held her back to his chest.

For a long, long time, they remained like that. Their chests moved in synchrony, their hearts beat as one, and they just... were.

It was everything Octavia wanted and more.

"Tell me a story?" Octavia murmured.

Lips brushed her cheeks. "About what?"

"Anything." Her eyes fluttered shut. "I just want to hear your voice."

She felt his smile as he kissed her ear. "It just so happens I know many stories. Did you ever hear about the Curse of the Black Thorn?"

"Never." She yawned.

"Once upon a time, in a forest far away, there lived a young Death Elf. She was born Without, but that didn't stop her from providing for her family. Her father was very ill, and…"

Flynn's voice was a quiet murmur, gently lulling Octavia to sleep as he spoke. She listened intently, asking quiet questions, as he wove his tale. Their words weren't barbed, and something shifted between them.

Slowly, she moved towards the realm of sleep.

"And they lived happily ever after," Flynn concluded softly.

"What a beautiful story," Octavia exhaled, so close to sleep that everything was heavy.

Several minutes passed in that quiet, comfortable calm.

Flynn's lips met her forehead. "This was nice. I wish it could always be like this between us."

The dragon shifter's brows furrowed, but before she could ask questions, sleep claimed her.

That night, her dreams were filled with sharp brown eyes and handsome witches who kissed like they were gods.

CHAPTER 7
A Multitude of Bad Choices

T he mattress beside Octavia was cold. She flung out her hand, wondering where Flynn had gone. He'd slept behind her all night, holding her tight against him.

She cracked her eyes open. It was still dark. Through the solitary window, she glimpsed the shifting sky. The sun was rising, pushing away the night with deep, scarlet tendrils of light. A shiver ran through the dragon shifter.

Red skies were never a good omen.

A rustling sound came from behind Octavia. That was strange. There wasn't much in the cabin. Just the bed, them, and her bag...

She inhaled sharply, and her fist clenched at her side.

There was no way Flynn was doing what she suspected, right? No one would be so cold as to betray someone like that, especially after the night they'd shared.

It was one thing to go through a stranger's bag, but after their kisses...

Her heart lodged in her throat as she slowly turned around. There had to be another explanation, right?

Like what? the dragon asked.

Anything.

Octavia needed her suspicions to be wrong. She needed to trust Flynn. She needed to...

Her eyes landed on the witch. A slew of vicious curses pulsed through her mind.

Right then and there, Octavia vowed to pry her heart out of her chest and never let anyone touch her again. Betrayal was bitter at the back of her mouth as she beheld the witch crouched over her bag, hurriedly searching through it.

Fucking bastard.

Fury was a blazing, burning inferno tearing through her veins. Red tinged everything in sight. Her nostrils flared. She flung herself out of bed so fast that she landed on her bad ankle. It rolled beneath her sudden weight, and she sucked in a sharp breath, alerting him to her presence.

The untrustworthy witch straightened. "Octavia—"

"What the hell do you think you're doing?" Octavia asked through clenched teeth.

The muscles in his back tightened, and his shoulders tensed. He dropped her bag and slowly turned around. "Beautiful, if you let me explain—"

Octavia punched him in the face.

His nose crunched on impact, and blood streamed from the wound.

"Fuck!" he shouted. His hands opened as they flew to cradle his broken nose, and something dropped to the ground with a *thunk* before it rolled under the bed.

All the air was sucked out of the room.

He looked at her. She looked at him. Their eyes grew three sizes larger at the same time.

Then he released his still-bleeding nose and dropped to the ground on all fours.

Octavia was faster. Even with her injured ankle, she got there before him. She groaned as she slammed onto the wooden planks, her foot screaming in pain, but it didn't matter. None of it mattered. Not the lying, thieving witch. Not the pain.

Just the object.

A glimmer of green caught her eye. It had rolled beneath the bed. She flattened herself and crawled beneath the mattress, ignoring the presence of dust and other questionable things.

"Octavia, please let me explain. It's not what you think," Flynn begged, his hand landing on her good foot.

She kicked him off. There was no explanation that could fix this. Whatever they'd had, he'd shattered it into a million pieces.

Ignoring the duplicitous witch, Octavia reached for her prize. She stretched her arm as far as it could go, twisting until her fingers closed around the cool emerald.

A breath of relief whooshed out of Octavia, and for a moment, she rested her head on the ground. She still had it. She couldn't lose it. If anything, the past twelve hours had taught her that witches were not the men for her.

She never should have kissed Flynn, never dreamed about him, never touched him. Clearly, her character judgement was seriously flawed.

Octavia wouldn't be making the same mistake twice.

Keeping a firm grip on the emerald, Octavia extricated herself from under the bed. Leaning on her good foot, she hobbled over to her bag and shoved her prize inside.

A hand landed on her shoulder. "Please, Octavia—"

"Don't!" Tears pricked behind her eyes, and she angrily huffed them back. "Don't fucking touch me. Last night was a mistake. This was all a mistake."

"No, you don't mean that."

"Don't tell me what I mean." She clutched the bag to her chest and turned around. "Tell me the truth: were you trying to steal the emerald?"

He bit his lip and clenched his jaw. In that split-second of silence that followed, she got her answer.

"Fuck. You." She shoved past him, limping to the door. Flynn called her name, but she ignored him as she yanked it open.

A guard stood on the other side. "Miss?"

"I'm ready to leave," she snapped. "Can I please have my walking stick back? I'm going *alone*."

She emphasized the last word, ignoring Flynn's hitched breath behind her. The guard must have seen something in her eyes because he did not argue.

Within half an hour, Octavia was on her way. Walking stick in hand, she trudged through the woods once more.

And damn it all, but even though he'd betrayed her, Octavia couldn't get Flynn out of her head.

FOUR DAYS PASSED in relative silence. Octavia hiked over hills and mountains. She'd long since stopped admiring the beauty around her. She was too tired for that. She was too tired for anything except putting one foot in front of the other.

Soreness had become her state of being. Every night, she stopped to massage her throbbing ankle when she found shelter beneath a tree or in a cave.

It wasn't an easy hike, but at least the rain didn't return.

Neither did Flynn.

Every so often, a branch cracked behind her, but when she looked, there was nothing there. The bag remained at Octavia's side, the emerald tucked deep within it.

On the fifth day, the shining sun greeted Octavia as she woke up. The air carried hints of salt, the dense woods thinned, and the crashing of waves against rocks grew louder by the hour. The Indigo Coast was near.

Excellent. A flutter of excitement bloomed in her stomach. It wouldn't be long before Octavia made her delivery, and then, finally, she'd be done.

Thank Kydona, the dragon growled. *The sooner we get rid of the object and shift, the better.*

The creature beneath Octavia's skin was getting testier with each passing day.

Octavia's mood wasn't faring much better. Flynn's betrayal had taught her an important lesson: she couldn't trust anyone.

Once she completed her mission, she'd be embarking upon a long vacation. She'd heard it snowed a lot in the north of the Rose Empire. Maybe she'd go explore some frozen lakes, far away from everyone else. Fire ran through her veins, and it would keep her warm.

Octavia was so entangled in her thoughts about what she'd like to do after she shifted that she didn't catch the change in the air.

One moment, the forest was filled with joyous birdsong, animals running around, and the wind rustling leaves. The next, absolute silence blanketed the woods.

The hairs on the back of Octavia's neck prickled, and she extended her senses.

"Hello?" she called out to the forest and turned in a slow circle, gripping her walking stick. "Is anyone there?"

A long moment of silence stretched on and on. A chill slinked down Octavia's spine, and a sense of wrongness filled her. Moving her walking stick from her right to her left hand, she took another step forward.

Then, the ground shifted beneath her feet.

One moment, she stood in front of an old, gnarled grandfather tree with brown bark. The next, bright emerald green vines snaking up the trunk. The speed with which they moved was incredibly unnatural until the vines swallowed up the tree.

Octavia shrieked and stumbled back. Or she would've, if dark green, almost black vines as thick as ropes weren't crawling up her legs. She batted at them and tried to get out, but for each one that she struck down, another two burst from the ground. They wound around her, climbing her just like the tree, until she couldn't possibly move anymore.

And with one swift tug, she ended up on the ground.

A flurry of curses so vile they could've curdled milk left Octavia's lips. Another vine rose and wrapped around her mouth, swallowing her cries of protest as she flailed against her bindings.

Only then did three figures, two with wings and one without, step out of the woods. Their pointed ears and the green ribbons of magic swirling around their fingers were further proof of what Octavia had already figured out. They were Earth Elves.

Unlike the purple wings of Octavia's dragon, the Earth Elves had pale green butterfly wings that fluttered behind them. The wings, though beautiful, did not mask the elves' viciousness. The males reeked of danger.

The wingless Earth Elf stepped forward. Green swirls and whorls Maturation tattoos were wrapped around his neck and exposed collarbone. They glowed as vividly as his grassy eyes. His dirty blond hair was cut ruggedly around his ears, and there was a dimple on his right cheek. He probably would have been handsome if not for the malice radiating from him or the smirk marring his face. The weapon hanging off his belt didn't help matters, either.

"Well, well," Wingless said. "Look what we've caught, brothers."

The winged elves wore matching smirks as they eyed Octavia.

"Is she a human, Lysandro?" the youngest-looking one asked, a spark of eagerness in his eyes that had Octavia wishing she had a weapon.

Wingless—Lysandro—moved closer to Octavia. He crouched beside her and sniffed the air as though she were a dog. "No." The surprise was evident in his voice. "She's definitely not mortal. She smells of..." He sniffed again. "Smoke and ash."

Octavia tried not to roll her eyes at that description. How incredibly basic. All dragon shifters smelled of smoke, but they had underlying scents. This Earth Elf clearly lacked Octavia's superior olfactory senses.

His grassy eyes met Octavia's, and she tried not to wince at the obvious threat of brutality in his gaze. He didn't look away, not as he ran his fingers over the rounded shell of her ear, nor as he touched her chin. She jerked her head up, slamming her forehead into his with all her might. The resounding crack filled her with deep satisfaction.

"Stupid whore." Lysandro pinned her down with an arm across the neck, and he bent, dragging his nose along her neck. "We've caught ourselves a dragon shifter, brothers."

The tone of his voice sent warning bells through Octavia. She struggled against the Earth Elf, but between the way he was pinning her and the vines, it was no use.

"Truly?" the middle brother asked.

"We're going to be rich," the other said excitedly.

Lysandro stared at Octavia as though he could see into her soul. "What are you doing so far east, poppet?"

She tried to hit him again.

He just laughed, easily evading her.

"I don't think she's going to tell you, brother," said the youngest. "Why don't you see what's in her bag?"

Alarm pulsed through Octavia. It was one thing for these malicious elves to know she was a dragon shifter, another entirely for them to question what she carried.

Shit. She was going to have to shift. She couldn't see any other way out of this. The Elders would be furious with her.

But they'd be even more angry if you lose the object, the dragon within Octavia rightly argued.

That was true. Better shift than die. She watched the elves carefully, bidding her time.

"We'll find out eventually." Lysandro rose to his feet and walked around Octavia. "We'll take her with us. I'm sure the fae will pay very well for a dragon shifter."

A scream crawled up Octavia's throat, swallowed by the gag around her mouth. Sell her to the fae? She trembled. Everyone knew that the fae who lived on the other of the Indigo Ocean were as cruel as vampires and known to collect exotic species from the Rose Empire as pets.

That would not happen. She didn't belong to anyone but herself.

As Lysandro bent, clearly intent on picking her up, the dragon shifter resigned herself to the Elders' wrath. Although, to be fair, they'd probably rather she shift than get herself shipped across the ocean. Or maybe they didn't care. That was a fucking depressing though, and Octavia frowned as she reached within herself for the shift.

The moment Lysandro touched her, she would let her dragon free.

Except... the Earth Elf's touch never came.

Bright, ribbons the color of a cloudless sky filled the forest like a swarm of bees. Lysandro's eyes widened, and he shouted. It didn't matter. The magic slammed into the three Earth Elves, and a *boom* echoed through the forest.

The Earth Elves' eyes bulged, and they grabbed at their necks, choking. One by one, the trio fell to their knees. A few long, drawn-out seconds later, they each collapsed on the ground, unconscious.

Octavia's heart raced. Her fingers clenched at the dirt, and she looked around as best she could for the source of the magic.

What were the chances there was another witch in the forest?

Slim, the dragon said.

That's what Octavia was afraid of. Her fingers curled in the fabric of the bag around her hip, and she gripped it as best she could through the vines holding her down.

"Flynn?" she called out, the words garbled by the gag, half-hoping she was wrong.

A heartbeat later, her fears were confirmed. Looking amazing for having hiked for days, Flynn stepped out from behind a tree. His cloak billowed behind him, and his sword hung from the scabbard at his hip. He must have gotten it back from the werewolves.

Flynn walked between the fallen elves until he made it to Octavia's side. He crouched, and his brows furrowed as he looked over the dragon shifter. Octavia looked him over as well. She couldn't help it. Her treacherous core twisted, remembering the way his lips had felt on hers. Her body didn't seem to care about his betrayal at all.

Why did he have to be the one who came to save her?

The witch moved with complete efficiency as he grabbed the knife attached to Lysandro's belt.

Octavia could do nothing but lie still as she watched the witch carefully. It bothered her that a small part of her was happy to see him. She was frustrated that he was here. Why couldn't he stay away?

Flynn severed the first vine around her feet with ease. "I'm sorry, Octavia." He cut another vine. "I shouldn't have done what I did."

A third vine went.

With each swipe of the blade, Flynn apologized. Not just for looking through her bag the second time but for everything he'd done. It was as if he'd been thinking about what he would say for days, because he repented of his numerous sins against her.

The problem—and it truly was a problem because Octavia wanted to hate Flynn for what he had done—was that the witch truly sounded contrite. Octavia had spent enough time around assholes that she could recognize them easily—and Flynn didn't strike her as one.

When he cut away the vine gagging her, she flexed her jaw and asked, "Why?"

That was the real question. Flynn could apologize all he wanted, but she needed to know the truth of the matter. If he couldn't give her that, then it didn't matter if he was contrite or not because it wouldn't work between them.

Flynn sucked in a deep breath, sawing at the thickest vines tangled around Octavia's feet.

"Did I ever tell you about Amyla?" he asked quietly, his eyes on his work.

Octavia stared at the witch. It seemed she'd been doing that a lot since he emerged from the woods. "No, you never mentioned her."

She would've remembered a beautiful name like that.

"That's what I thought." Flynn's voice was soft and carried traces of wistfulness. He worked silently for a few minutes, his eyes glazed as though he was remembering something from long ago.

"Last one," he murmured. "Hold still."

She was as still as the logs around her as he sawed at the largest vine holding her down. When it snapped, she exhaled, a feeling of relief washing over her.

She was free.

Flynn clambered to his feet and reached out a hand in offering. After a moment, Octavia took it, and he helped her stand.

"Amyla is my youngest sister," he said.

"Youngest?"

He nodded. "I have five. Amyla is... well, she's not yet Mature, and she's... naïve."

Octavia drew her bottom lip through her teeth. She wasn't exactly sure where Flynn was going with this, nor how it pertained to him trying to steal from her, but she was willing to hear him out. "Oh?"

The witch picked up Octavia's walking stick and handed it to her. "About a year ago, Amyla got caught up with some bad people."

A pit formed in Octavia's stomach. She had a sense of where this story was going, and it wasn't good. A large part of her wanted to tell Flynn to stop, to keep the words to himself, but she didn't. Somehow, she knew she needed to hear this.

Flynn looked over at Octavia, and darkness flitted through his eyes. "Amyla should've known better than to get involved. I warned her. So did my parents. But sometimes—"

"People make bad choices," Octavia finished his sentence.

After all, she was familiar with those. She'd made quite a few when it came to Flynn, but she couldn't seem to stop. She was drawn to him.

"Yes." Flynn nodded, taking Octavia's elbow and leading her away from the fallen Earth Elves. "We should go. They're not dead, but they'll wake up with the headache of their lives and no memory of the last day."

Gratitude was a river of cool water running through Octavia. "Thank you," she said, realizing she hadn't done so yet. "For coming, for saving me..."

"Don't thank me," he said gruffly, running his free hand through his hair. "I shouldn't have... I didn't... don't. Just don't."

Octavia frowned, but she didn't argue as Flynn guided her out of the clearing. They hiked in silence for several minutes as the crashing of waves against rocks grew louder. Soon, the deep blue, almost purple, water of the Indigo Ocean was visible through the trees.

"So your sister..." Octavia glanced at Flynn. "What happened?"

"She got entangled with some extremely dangerous people." Flynn sighed. "She's in over her head, and I'm trying to buy her out. The thing is, it's very expensive."

Understanding was dawning on Octavia. "I see."

She stopped, reaching into her bag. Her fingers closed around the emerald. She took a deep breath, hoping she was doing the right thing, before pulling out the object. Glimmering in the light of the afternoon sun, the flower fit perfectly in Octavia's palm. It hummed faintly, carrying traces of powerful magic.

The Emerald Rose.

The Elders had entrusted it to Octavia. She had no idea where it came from or what it did, but she knew it was important.

"Who told you about the rose?" she murmured.

Flynn cleared his throat. "The people who have Amyla are part of an underground network of thieves. They had information that someone would be delivering the rose to the coast. I figured..."

His voice trailed off, and he fidgeted.

Octavia sighed, sensing she knew where this was going. "You were going to steal the flower and use the proceeds to pay for your sister's release?"

He nodded mutely, his mouth twisting as regret and shame dueled on his face.

Damn it all. Why couldn't Flynn just have been some no-good thief? Why did he have to have such a strong, noble reason for wanting to steal the rose?

A burdensome sigh left Flynn's lips, and his shoulders sagged. "I'm sorry, Octavia." His chin dipped, and his head hung low. "I should never have tried to steal the rose. Especially not once I... when we... connected the way we did."

That was an interesting way to describe what had happened in the werewolf's guest house.

"No, you shouldn't have." Dropping the rose back in her bag, Octavia groaned and ran her hands through her hair. At least, she tried. In reality, her fingers got stuck in her black curls. Fucking great. Of course they did.

Wiggling them free, she paced back and forth as best she could, using her walking stick for leverage.

She'd never encountered a situation like this in Firefall. Her first instinct was anger—to yell and tell him it was too late, that she couldn't forgive him because he'd tried to steal the rose not once, but twice.

The difficulty was that she heard the ringing of truth in his voice. The pain lacing his words was real, and it pulled on Octavia's heart strings.

"Damn it all," she growled. "You were really just trying to help your sister?"

How could she hate him for trying to help his family? Octavia would like to believe that if she had someone in her life who needed as much help as it seemed Flynn's sister did, she would do anything to help them.

"Yes, I was, but... I can't. I won't." Flynn reached out as though to touch Octavia before seeming to think better of it. He dropped his hand in the space between them. "I can't do that to you. Because..."

His voice trailed off, and he gestured between the two of them.

Octavia's breath caught in her throat.

"What are you saying?" She thought she knew, but... how could this be?

"I wasn't sure at first. Or maybe I was, but I didn't want to admit it. I can't ignore it anymore. I shouldn't have ignored it at all." Flynn's piercing gaze met hers, and her legs knocked together at the intensity in his eyes. "There's a connection between us."

Octavia's heart slammed at the witch's words. Even now, her body thrummed from the witch's nearness. The crashing of the waves behind them was nothing compared to the racing of her heart in his presence.

"We barely know each other," she said, pointing out the obvious.

He nodded. "I know."

"You lied and tried to steal from me. Twice."

"I know. I don't deserve your forgiveness, but I would do anything to earn it."

His words made her heart beat even faster.

"This is ridiculous. Foolish, even." Still, she stepped closer to him.

"Probably." He approached her slowly.

There was a foot between them, maybe less.

Everything else faded away. The crashing of the nearby waves, the birds flying overhead, the rays of sunlight shining upon them.

Nothing else mattered but them.

"There's really only one reason this could be happening," Octavia admitted. "It seems unlikely, but—"

"You're my mate," Flynn whispered, sounding like he could barely believe the words.

The words hung in the air between them, ringing with truth. Something deep within Octavia shifted, and a *rightness* that she'd never felt before settled upon her.

Three long, eternal seconds passed in complete silence.

Then, she whispered his name at the same time that he said hers.

He hugged her, drawing her close as their mouths crashed together. The kiss was desperate and powerful, urgent and right. It was *everything*.

Sparks ran through the dragon shifter. Her heart sped up. She dropped her walking stick, and her fingers grappled in his shirt. Stars shone in her vision.

Flynn groaned. The sound was unlike anything Octavia had ever heard. Her toes curled, and she leaned into the witch. She closed her eyes and gave herself into this embrace.

They kissed and kissed.

Octavia couldn't believe that she had a mate, and it was *Flynn*.

Wait.

Flynn.

Despite the pleasure coursing through her, Octavia's eyes flew open. They couldn't do this. Not right now. They had problems to solve.

The lying, for one. The emerald rose, for another. Adding a mate to the mix would further complicate things. They'd have to deal with this later.

Reluctantly, Octavia broke their embrace. She shook her head. "We can't do this."

Flynn's eyes momentarily widened, then shuttered. "Okay." He took a deep breath. "I... understand. I lied to you, and just because I rescued you doesn't mean you can forgive me. That's fair. I don't... I understand." He stepped away from her and dipped his head. "Stay safe, Octavia Ashbloom."

He turned, but not before she glimpsed the silver shining in his eyes.

Octavia watched Flynn go, her heart growing heavier with each step he took. She let him take fifteen paces before she took pity on him.

"Wait," she called out.

Instantly, he froze. His back was to her, the muscles tense as he stood, a statue in front of the Indigo Ocean.

Octavia bent and picked up her walking stick. The tension in the air was palpable as she moved towards the witch. When she was close enough, she placed her hand on his shoulder.

Flynn drew in a deep breath.

Octavia knew with certainty that, at that moment, she could drive a wedge between them that was so deep they would never recover. She could wound this man with her words, make him forever regret what he'd done to her.

Or she could pick a different path. One that would alter the rest of their lives.

She drew in a deep breath, closed her eyes for the briefest moment, and then she made up her mind.

CHAPTER 8
Red Stars are Falling

"I don't want you to leave," Octavia said, the words coming out softer than she'd intended.

Flynn turned around slowly, as if he was afraid this was a dream. His fists clenched and unclenched at his sides. "You don't?"

The bewilderment on his face was such a far cry from the cocky, too-handsome witch Octavia had gotten used to over the past couple of weeks that it was almost funny.

She shook her head. "No."

His brows knit together. "But you said—"

"We can't keep kissing, even though I'd love to do that, because we have things to do." Octavia pointed in the direction of the Earth Elves they'd left behind. "I don't know about you, but I don't want to be here when they wake up."

Another moment passed as Flynn's brown gaze flicked over Octavia. She saw the moment he realized what she was saying because his eyes lit up.

"You mean you're not rejecting me?" He sounded incredulous.

Honestly, Octavia was surprised, too. But the more she thought about it, the better she felt about her decision.

"No, I'm not."

"Why not?" Bewilderment was etched on his face.

Why indeed? There were several reasons, but the most important one was that despite everything, Octavia *liked* Flynn. A lot. She could see herself being with him for a long time. It didn't mean she would accept their mate bond right then and there—it required consent from both sides—but she wanted to see where this relationship could go.

And as for the lying and stealing, she understood where he was coming from. He was trying to save his sister. How could she blame him for that?

Octavia didn't say that, though. It seemed a little heavy for the moment. Instead, she grinned at the witch and started moving along the coast.

"I like looking at you," she informed him over her shoulder. "It would be a shame never to see your face again."

The corner of his lip twitched upwards. "I didn't know you were so superficial."

Octavia snorted and returned her gaze in front of her. "Apparently, I am."

Also, there was the added benefit that having a mate meant she wouldn't be alone any longer. After decades of being an outcast, she really liked that idea.

Flynn caught up with her, not that it was difficult, and he brushed his knuckles against hers. "You're quite beautiful yourself, Lady Octavia."

That again. This time, though, it didn't bother her as much. Or maybe it was just her opinion of the witch that was changing.

Either way, as they strolled along the coast, she felt lighter than she had in years.

After a few minutes, Flynn asked, "So, what's the plan?"

Octavia patted the bag. "Now, we go to Riverton and find Winnifred Black. Then, once I've made my delivery, we'll get the rest of the money you need and rescue your sister."

The witch didn't ask where they would get the funds from, and Octavia didn't tell him. Let him wonder for a bit. If he didn't already suspect what she was, he'd know the moment she shifted once the Elders' restrictions were lifted.

Flynn exhaled. "Thank you, Octavia."

She wasn't sure what he was thanking her for. Not rejecting him? Not telling him to leave? Or just for... understanding?

Either way, Octavia dipped her head. "Of course." She glanced over at him. "You're my mate."

Even though they hadn't sealed their bond, even though she wasn't sure they would, that connection lay between them.

And for the first time in over five decades, Octavia felt at peace.

———

THE SCENTS OF SALT, sex, and alcohol slammed into Octavia the moment they stepped into The Crystal Plate. Like most taverns in the Rose Empire, it also doubled as a brothel. Moans of pleasure intermingled with the clicking of utensils on dishes and the murmur of conversation. It was the middle of the day, and several round tables were unoccupied.

Three days had passed since the incident with the Earth Elves. They hadn't run into any other trouble on their way to Riverton, nor had she and Flynn broached the topic of their mateship again. But at night, he held her close, and she slept soundly.

This morning, Octavia's ankle had been inflamed when she woke. Flynn had used his magic to ease the pain, and her foot had felt better than it had in years. She vowed to get another brace made, but she couldn't deny the benefits of having a witch around.

Each day, Octavia was getting more comfortable with the idea of having a mate. Things with Flynn were simple and easy, and she liked that a lot.

The pair strode to the bar at the back.

"Can I help you?" The bartender, a muscular bald human, put down the glass he was cleaning.

Octavia nodded. "Yes, please. I need to see Mrs. Black." Flynn's hand was a steady presence on her back, and his touch grounded her. She added, "It's urgent."

"What do you want with Mrs. Black?" The bartender crossed his arms and stared them down.

"I have a delivery for her." Octavia tried not to let the man's questions irritate her, but she'd come so far and done so much. She just wanted to finish this and move on with her life.

"What if I told you she's indisposed?" the man asked.

"Then we would wait." The dragon shifter adjusted her weight, standing on her good foot. "Please tell her Octavia Ashbloom is here for her. Dawn is early, and the night is short."

The last sentence was a signal that the Elders had forced Octavia to memorize before she left.

The bartender stiffened when he heard it, and his fingers curled on the countertop. Three long seconds passed before he nodded. "Alright. Stay here." He turned and stomped up the stairs before disappearing from sight.

Come to think of it, maybe Octavia should have used the code phrase right away.

She glanced at Flynn. "He seems..."

"Grumpy," her witch said, nuzzling her neck. "You did great."

When had she started thinking of the witch as hers? Octavia wasn't certain, but she liked it. It felt *right*, in the same way that when Flynn held her, she felt safe. She'd never had that before. It was like her soul recognized his as a haven.

"Thank you," Octavia murmured.

Footsteps pounded on the stairs. The bartender stopped halfway down, gripping the railing for balance. "She'll see you."

A flash of blue slipped from Flynn's palms. It was so quick that Octavia was fairly certain no one else noticed, but she did. The fact that he was pulling magic, just in case something went wrong, was sweet. Little did he know that once she shifted, *she* would be the one protecting them.

She couldn't wait to see the look of surprise on his face when she finally showed him her dragon form. She still hadn't told him what she was, although he likely suspected it, but that would soon change.

Flynn laced their fingers together as they followed the bartender up the rickety stairs, and Octavia leaned against him.

Once they reached the second level, the dual purpose of the building was even clearer. From a room on the left came a trio of muffled cries—two females and a male, by the sounds of it—and from another, someone begged loudly for release. The room on the right simply boasted the rhythmic pounding of a headboard against the wall.

Octavia's cheeks flushed, and her grip tightened on Flynn's hand. This place, with its sounds and scents of desire, only amplified the feelings she already had for the witch.

Soon, she promised herself.

Once the rose was out of her hands, she would find out whether Flynn was as skilled in other departments as he was at kissing.

The bartender led them to a door at the back of the hallway. "Mrs. Black is very busy." He paused with his hand on the knob. "Make it quick."

Octavia nodded, and the human knocked twice.

"Enter," an ancient, wizened voice called out.

The bartender opened the door and stepped back, revealing a dimly lit office. A single armchair faced the hearth. Where a blazing fire should have been, a few logs smoldered.

"Come here, child."

Exchanging a glance with Flynn, Octavia let go of his hand and stepped around the chair. Bright blue eyes met hers, set in a face lined with age. It was impossible to see where one wrinkled ended, and the next began. Long snow-white hair flowed down to the woman's waist, hiding her ears from sight. A heavy black gown covered her from neck to toe like a blanket of death.

"Winnifred Black?" Octavia asked, gripping her messenger bag with one hand and her walking stick with the other.

What were the chances the bartender was playing a game with

her? This woman looked like she was moments away from Fading. How could she be the one Octavia sought?

"I am she," the woman said, her voice aged and so quiet that the dragon shifter strained to hear her.

"Dawn is coming, and the night is short," Octavia repeated the signal. She just... needed to be sure.

Those piercing blue eyes sharpened. "Red stars are falling, and death is on the horizon," the woman finished.

Octavia's shoulders incrementally relaxed. That was the sentence she'd been expecting. "I have the rose."

Winnifred's eyes shimmered, and for a moment, decades seemed to fall away from her face. "Finally," she breathed. "I have waited many years for this moment." She raised a gnarled hand. "Give me the flower."

Power infused those last words, and the air crackled.

Questions filled Octavia's mind. Who was this woman, and what did the rose do? She hadn't given it much thought before, but now she couldn't help but wonder. It was too late for those types of questions, though. She was a messenger, and this was her duty. Reaching into her bag, her fingers closed around the rose.

For a single moment, after she pulled it out, Octavia paused and studied the object. The glimmering emerald was cool to the touch, and she didn't sense any magic coming from the object. But there was a hum...

That moment's pause was too much for the old woman.

"Hand it over, little girl." Winnifred lurched out of her chair with far more agility than someone who looked so breakable should have had. Her fingers wrapped around Octavia's wrist, and she snatched the rose. The old woman traced the flower's edges and murmured something unintelligible beneath her breath.

"Mrs. Black?" Octavia glanced at the older woman. "What does the rose *do*?"

The old woman's head jerked up, and a flash of something dark and devious ran through her eyes. "None of your business, messenger," she snarled. "It's mine."

So, it was. Octavia supposed it didn't really matter. The Elders had commanded her to deliver the rose, and she'd done exactly that.

"Jacobs!" Winnifred called out.

The door opened, and the bartender entered. "Yes, ma'am?"

"Pay them, please." The old woman went back to admiring the rose, her dismissal obvious.

Jacobs jerked his head. Octavia exchanged a glance with Flynn, who raised a brow. He seemed to say, *I'll follow your lead.*

She could push for more information about the rose, but something told her it wasn't a good idea.

After a moment, Octavia nodded and followed Flynn out of the room. As the door slipped shut, she could've sworn she heard the old woman crooning to the rose.

"Downstairs," Jacobs said.

Apparently, the man wasn't much of a talker. He practically bounded down the steps before disappearing around the corner. Flynn went next, leaving Octavia to make her way down the steps. Avoiding putting too much weight on her bad ankle, she took the stairs at a much slower pace, careful about where she placed her feet. All this hiking was taking a toll on her, whether she cared to admit it or not.

But now your duty is complete, the dragon reminded Octavia. *Finally, we can take to the skies once more.*

Excitement was a flurry of tiny dragon wings in Octavia's stomach. The idea of flying again thrilled her. The way the air felt beneath her wings, the taste of the clouds, the—

Octavia yelped as her foot slipped on the third-to-last stair. She grabbed the railing, her heart thundering as she fought to remain upright. The rail cracked and split from the wall. It wasn't a clean break, and Octavia flailed. She tried to find something else to hold onto, but nothing was there.

She teetered forward, her hands grasping at empty air. Oh gods. She careened towards the floor. A fall, even one much worse than this, wouldn't kill a dragon. Very little could do that. But it would fucking hurt.

Octavia was mentally bracing herself for the inevitable onslaught of pain when a pair of hands landed on her hips.

"Careful, beautiful," Flynn rumbled as he lifted her down the steps and placed her on the ground beside him. "You wouldn't want to injure that gorgeous face of yours."

She was unharmed. Thanks to Flynn. She turned to him and dipped her head. "Thank you. You saved me twice now."

"I suppose I did," Flynn said.

"Thank you," she repeated. Her gaze dropped to where his hands were still on her hips. She made no move to pull away.

His thumb brushed a path along her side. She hitched a breath, and the rest of the tavern faded away until it was just the two of them.

Flynn's eyes darkened, and his head lowered. "I'm really sorry I tried to steal the rose," he murmured, his voice so low only she could hear it.

Octavia's gaze searched his for any sign that he was lying, and she didn't find one. Reaching up, she cupped his cheek. He pressed his face into her palm, his stubble tickling the tender flesh of her hand. "I believe you," she breathed. "And I accept your apology."

His hands tightened around her hips, and hope flashed through his eyes. "Does that mean—"

"I'm not sure if I'm ready to accept the bond, but... I'm willing to try. I want to know what *we* would be like." Octavia bit her lip, suddenly realizing she probably should have asked him if that's what he wanted. "I mean, if you... if we..."

His forehead pressed against hers. "Yes," he whispered. "I want to know what we'd be like. Together. I want you, no matter what."

Octavia exhaled, "Thank Kydona."

Flynn's eyes searched hers, and his mouth dipped lower and lower. Octavia's core twisted, and warmth ran through her.

He breathed her name, his breath dancing over her mouth as he moved slowly. Leisurely. As if they had all the time in the world.

Their lips were a hairsbreadth apart when he murmured, "I want to kiss you."

Yes, she got that.

"Please," she groaned. The anticipation was killing her.

A dark chuckle rumbled through him. "Are you eager, Octavia?"

"I am," she whispered. "And you're a tease."

"I—"

Someone coughed behind them. All of a sudden, Octavia remembered their surroundings. They weren't alone, and from the way several people were staring at them, they were apparently causing a bit of a scene.

Blood rushed to Octavia's cheeks as she stepped back from Flynn. With a scowl painted on his face, the bartender held out a bag of jingling coins in Octavia's direction. "Your payment." Jacobs raised a brow. "Do you require a room?"

Oh gods. If Octavia thought she was embarrassed before, that was nothing compared to how she felt now.

Accepting the payment, she laced her fingers through Flynn's once again and adjusted her grip on the walking stick. "I, uh... no, thank you."

They had other things to do, places to be, and sisters to save.

CHAPTER 9

A Gods-Damned Force to be Reckoned With

After procuring lunch from a street vendor—questionable roasted spiced meat and crusty bread—Octavia and Flynn wandered through Riverton and explored the city on the edge of the coast before heading to a clearing not far from town.

It was late afternoon, and the air carried a hint of impending rain as they came to a stop. For once, Octavia didn't mind the storm making its way towards them.

They wouldn't be here long enough for it to bother them.

"Where's Amyla being held?" she asked, taking her bag off and placing it on the ground beside her.

Flynn's eyes darkened, and blue sparks flitted off his hands. "Sandhaven," he growled, his voice deeper than Octavia had ever heard it. "The Desert City."

Octavia's eyes widened. Located on the southern edge of the Rose Empire, Sandhaven was one of the largest cities in the Rose Empire, second only to the capital of Blackrose, home to the Emerald Empress. Octavia had never been to Sandhaven, but she'd heard of it.

"There's an... *establishment* there. Like a brothel, but... worse," Flynn seethed. Anger flashed through his eyes. While he might not have any dragon fire running through his veins, evidently, he could be fierce when he wanted to. "If I don't get there by the next full moon, they will sell her as a slave."

A knot twisted in Octavia's stomach. Dragon shifters didn't keep slaves, but others did. She had heard horrific rumors about the way they were treated, especially by the Emerald Empress.

"Remind me how much you need to buy her freedom?" Flynn named the number, and Octavia nodded, making a few calculations in her head. The proceeds from the Emerald Rose would cover most of that, and the rest wouldn't be difficult to come by. "Alright, that's doable. We can be there by tomorrow evening."

Flynn stared at her. "Octavia, it takes three weeks to reach Sandhaven on horseback. Unless you know a vampire who can shadow us there, there's no way we can be there tomorrow."

"I think you'll see that's not true." Eager to share her surprise, Octavia handed Flynn the bag of money.

His brows knit together. "Is there a plan you want to..."

The rest of his words never came. Octavia unceremoniously dropped her cloak and bag on the ground. She pulled her tunic over her head, leaving her in just a white band wrapped around her breasts. The witch's gaze dropped to her chest, and he swallowed.

Octavia couldn't help it. She smirked at the surprised expression on his face. He was about to get even more shocked.

"Yes, there's a plan, and no, I'm not like most people." Octavia's hands went around her back, and she quickly undid the knot that kept the band in place. "I can get us to Sandhaven by tomorrow, we just need to make a stop first."

"I... uh..." Flynn's eyes bulged as Octavia let the band fall to the ground.

Apparently, the witch's linguistic capabilities were greatly hampered by nudity. Octavia would have to keep that in mind. She wouldn't deny that it was rather enjoyable, seeing the handsome witch struggle to find words in the face of a bit of flesh. Shifters had no problems being nude.

If Flynn couldn't speak now, he would really have a problem in a moment. Octavia's hands went to her leggings, and she pulled them off without hesitation.

Flynn did his best impression of a bug. His eyes bulged, and he rubbed his hand over his face. "You... naked," he rasped. "Why? I mean... beautiful, but..."

Octavia laughed as she gathered her clothes and wrapped them in her cloak. "Very astute of you to notice. Now, be a dear and hold these for me?"

The witch's movements were stiff as he took the clothes. His eyes never left hers. If he were anyone else, Octavia would be angry with him by the way he was looking, but Flynn...

The fire in his gaze had nothing to do with anger and everything to do with *her*. The way he looked at her made her feel beautiful and strong, and she loved that.

Maybe this mate business had benefits Octavia had yet to consider.

She took a step back. "You know how to ride, right?"

"I... yes. I've ridden a horse."

"Good. This is kind of like that." In the loosest possible way. At least, that's what she'd been told.

Flynn's brows creased, but before he could speak, Octavia closed her eyes and reached for her magic.

Is it time? The dragon was eager.

It is, Octavia confirmed.

Drawing on the shift was as easy as breathing. Octavia released the hold she kept around the dragon, letting her magic flood through her. A flash of light erupted from within her, coating the clearing in white.

It didn't matter that she hadn't shifted for years. This was what she was born to do. She and the dragon were one. Their souls were merged at their core. All shifters were born with the innate ability to access their inner creatures, and dragons were no different.

Handing the reigns over to the dragon felt like taking a deep breath for the first time in years. Octavia's bones cracked and reformed, her neck elongated, her wings burst from her back, and her fingers stretched into long talons.

In her two-legged form, Octavia's ankle always bothered her, even on the best days. But when she shifted, she didn't feel the pain at all. The injury was still there, but it didn't impede her dragon's movements.

Finally, she was completely, fully herself.

Octavia spread her wings, letting the feeling of this form ground her once again as the light faded.

"A fucking dragon," Flynn whispered.

The words would've been too quiet for Octavia to hear in her regular form, but now it was as if he'd shouted them in her ear. When she was shifted, everything was brighter. More vibrant and vivid. Scents were sharper. Sounds were louder. Needs were stronger.

Octavia stared at Flynn through slitted eyes. That he hadn't run screaming in the other direction seemed like a good sign.

Placing the bundle of clothes on the ground, Flynn extended a hand and carefully approached. "Are you... can I touch you?"

There was a hint of nervousness in the witch's voice that was new. Octavia liked that, possibly more than she was willing to admit.

It reminded her that her dragon was strong and powerful. In this form, she wasn't just a woman to be pushed around by men. She was a gods-damned force to be reckoned with.

Spreading her wings, the tips brushing the trees on either side, Octavia nodded and lowered her head to the ground. From her peripheral vision, she could just make out the vivid amethyst of her wings. Octavia had always loved the way her dragon looked. Some dragons were green or blue, which were nice colors, but purple was different. Better, in her opinion. It was a rich, beautiful color that made her feel as special as the Emerald Empress herself.

Flynn gulped, his eyes widening as he extended a hand. To his eternal credit, he didn't tremble. That was more than Octavia could say for far older, Mature males she'd encountered in the past.

The moment the witch's fingers touched Octavia's snout, his lips twitched up into a smile. Flynn was always handsome, but when he was happy, it was a sight to behold.

"You are magnificent, Octavia," he breathed, awe tinging his every word.

She snorted and rubbed her much larger nose against his hand.

The laugh that burst out of him warmed Octavia more than the fire in her veins. It was deep and rich, like a warm hug after a cold day in the rain.

There was a part of Octavia that had been afraid that when Flynn saw her like this, he would not want her. She hadn't even admitted it to herself until now. The fact that he was not scared of her meant everything.

Flynn circled Octavia, running his hand over her scales. She was an enormous, purple statue as he touched her wings, her flank, and even the spikes on her tail. She focused on her breathing, knowing that even one wrong move could accidentally hurt him. His touch was gentle but strong, just like the man she'd come to know over the past few weeks.

He returned to her front and met one of Octavia's slitted eyes. "Can you speak when you're shifted?"

She shook her head. Dragons could communicate mind to mind with each other while shifted, but she couldn't speak to him. That was reserved to select mated pairs.

Maybe they would be able to do it in the future... if they accepted their bond.

She met his gaze, silently asking, *Is that going to be a problem?*

He must have understood her question, because he shook his head.

"No, I trust you." Flynn gathered her clothes and stuffed them in her bag. Adjusting his sword, he asked, "Can I... ride you?"

She dipped her head.

"Alright. Here I go, riding a dragon. My mate is a dragon."

Maybe Flynn wasn't taking this as well as it initially seemed. He approached her without trepidation though, and his movements were steady as he climbed up her front leg. He settled in front of Octavia's wings, his thighs locking around her.

After giving Flynn time to situate himself, Octavia lifted her head to check on the witch. He sat on her back proudly, her bag secured over his shoulder. He appeared natural, like he'd been born to ride. He caught her eye and nodded as if to say, *I'm ready*.

The plan was simple.

One of Octavia's hoards was a few hours' flight away. It was—presumably—untouched. They'd go there first, and then once they had secured the money they needed, they would leave for Sand-haven first thing in the morning.

She roared, the sound shaking the leaves of the nearby trees, and launched into the sky.

The first moments of the flight were glorious. Being unable to shift had been akin to torture, and Octavia was finally free. She swooped through the afternoon sky, careful not to dislodge the witch on her back.

Freedom tasted like the warm summer air, and it felt like home. Finally, she was liberated from the shackles of her mistake.

Bellowing in delight, Octavia spread her wings and *flew*.

CHAPTER 10
A Dragon's Hoard and Other Things

Several hours later, Octavia spotted her cave in the distance. Decades had passed since her last visit, but hopefully, her treasure was still untouched. After all, she'd paid a witch an indecent sum of money to ward it.

All dragons in the Rose Empire had hoards. It was in their blood. Most people assumed that because the dragons lived in villages like Firefall, they were poor, but that wasn't the case. They pooled resources and ensured everyone was looked after, but each dragon's treasure belonged to them.

In theory, everyone was cared for, and no one was lonely. It was just a fucking theory, though. The past few decades had taught Octavia that loneliness could still exist even when someone was surrounded by people.

But she wasn't lonely anymore.

Roaring, she banked her wings and hoped that Flynn was holding on tight. She angled towards the ground and touched down smoothly right in front of the cave entrance. A perfect landing.

Thumping her tail on the ground, Octavia patiently waited as Flynn slipped off her back.

He moved in front of her and studied the mountain. An

opening just large enough for two people was cut into the mountainside. "It's a...cave." He lifted a brow. "Is this... your cave?"

She nodded. She claimed it after her very first messenger job. She'd delivered a missive to Lord Caron, a high-ranking noble of the Emerald Court. The lord had paid Octavia handsomely, and once she'd outfitted the cave, she'd hired a local witch to enchant it for her.

If Flynn tried to enter it now, he would be stopped by magic. Hopefully, he would wait. Octavia had no desire to see what would happen if someone tried to enter the cave without her dismantling the wards. This was one of those moments where it would've been helpful if she could communicate with Flynn while she was in this form.

Lifting her head, she gestured for Flynn to back up. He did, intrigue filling his eyes.

Octavia pulled on the shift and let the rapid change come over her. By the time she stood on her two legs, Flynn had fished out her clothes and held them out to her with his eyes squeezed shut. That was an unexpected, albeit unnecessary, sweet gesture.

"Thank you," she murmured and took the clothes.

"Always."

Gods, why did that one word sound like a promise?

Octavia took her time as she dressed, taking advantage of the opportunity to look over her witch. Maybe it was the bond between them, or maybe it was something else, but she was drawn to him more with each passing day.

Flynn stood still, the slight movement of his chest the only sign that he was alive. His reddish-brown hair was disheveled from the flight, his cheeks were red, his lips were as kissable as ever, and his eyelashes were long.

The dragon shifter stood by her initial assessment of the witch —he was far too handsome for his own good. The difference between now and their first meeting was that this time, Octavia didn't mind his handsomeness.

Not. At. All.

"I'm decent," she said as she drew her curly black hair out of the tunic's collar. "Can I borrow your sword?"

Flynn's brows shot up as he opened his eyes. "Uh, sure." He slid the weapon out of its sheath, his muscles rippling with the movement. "Here."

Accepting the blade, she held the hilt with one hand and sliced her other palm against the sharpened steel.

"What the fuck?" Flynn snarled.

She handed him the blade, her dripping blood staining the grass red as she studied the cave entrance. "Relax, I'm fine."

"You're bleeding!" Panic sharpened his voice. "By definition, that's not fine."

His concern was admirable, and Octavia's heart swelled. "It's okay. I'll heal. I just need to find the key to the blood ward..."

Her voice trailed off as she found the rock she was looking for. She crouched, placing her bleeding palm on the gray shale. The gentle hum of magic crawled over her skin like an endless brush of feathers. Several heartbeats passed before the air shifted.

"There." Octavia straightened and flexed her palm. A dull pain was present, but her hand was already healing. There were benefits to being a Mature dragon shifter, after all. She reached over and laced her fingers through his. "Hold on, this shouldn't hurt."

"Wait. Shouldn't?"

They were already through the entrance by the time Flynn finished speaking. The ward ran over her like water, but they were both able to step through. That was good. She would hate if her mate were hurt because of something she did.

Exhaling, Octavia released his hand and grabbed the gnarled walking stick she'd left here. "Come on, Flynn. It's safe."

He hesitated for a mere moment before nodding. "I trust you. Lead the way."

Octavia did just that, the rhythmic tapping of her walking stick against the shale like the beat of a steady drum as they headed into the cave. The ceiling was maybe ten feet high, and from the front, it appeared no different from the hundreds of caves that dotted the eastern portion of the Rose Empire. Stone walls rose above them, dirt and debris were under their feet, and a few stray pine needles and leaves carpeted the ground.

"So, this is your cave," Flynn remarked as Octavia led him around a corner.

She nodded. "Mhmm. One of them."

His arm brushed hers, sending jolts of awareness running through her. "How many do you have?"

"A few," Octavia said, her response non-committal. She would see how he reacted to this one before she told him about the others.

She had five, but some dragons had upwards of twenty hoards. It was a natural side effect of living for a long time and working as messengers. Dragons loved treasure, and they did whatever they could to keep it for themselves.

"That's..." Whatever Flynn planned to say never came because they turned the last corner. He stopped in his tracks and breathed her name. "This is... wow."

Although lacking in eloquence, Octavia thought that was a good way to describe this hoard. It was her favorite, and she was pleased to see that everything was untouched, just as she'd left it.

Mine, the dragon growled.

Glowing clusters of blue and green luminescent mushrooms were scattered through the inner portion of the cavern, casting their light on the treasure. Three piles of shimmering gold coins were clumped together. Jewels glimmered. In the furthest corner from the entrance, a crimson velvet couch sat next to a gilded trunk. Those had been Octavia's most recent additions before her unexpected absence.

Giving Flynn time to appreciate the riches laid out before him, Octavia made her way over to the couch and perched on the armrest. She watched with dragon pride as the witch admired her glittering stash.

If they were to accept the mating bond, Flynn needed to know Octavia was a dragon through and through. Dragons cared for three things in life: family, flying, and riches. The Elders' punishment had stripped Octavia of not one but two of these things. She would not allow either of those things to be taken from her again.

Several minutes passed before the witch raked a hand through his hair. His back was to her as he studied the pile of coins closest to him. "This is... you really are a lady, aren't you?"

Octavia scoffed. "No, I'm not. Dragons don't have lords and ladies. Ranks are not important to us."

Except for the Elders. They were the dragons' version of a government. The Emerald Empress ruled over the continent, and the dragons submitted to her laws because it would be too much work to rise against her, but for the most part, they remained on their own.

"Okay. You're not a lady," Flynn said.

Finally, he was getting it. She'd only been telling him that from the moment they met.

"No," Octavia murmured. "Does that bother you?"

She hoped it didn't. But if it did, it was better to get that out of the way now. She could already feel herself growing attached to the witch. If he was going to leave her because she wasn't a lady, she'd rather he do it now before she did something utterly stupid like give him her heart, only for him to turn around and break it. That would possibly be even worse than everything else she had already endured.

"Not at all." Flynn's voice was deep as it echoed through the cavern. He turned and strode towards her, his steps sire and his eyes gleaming. Truth rang from his every word. "You could be a scullery maid, and I wouldn't care. I want you, Octavia."

The look in his eyes was dark and filled with something she wasn't quite ready to label.

Those three words echoed all around them.

I want you.

When was the last time someone had wanted her? She couldn't remember hearing them, at least not recently.

Her heart pounded in her chest, her breath caught in her throat, and she rose from the couch. "Truly?"

She couldn't stop the ember of hope that sparked in her core. It was one thing to have a mate. Those were predestined by the fates. It was another thing entirely to be wanted by someone. Octavia didn't realize how much she desired it until he said those words.

Seconds stretched on.

Although she told herself it was foolish, she couldn't stop the hope from growing brighter within her. Gods, she prayed he would not take those words back. Did he realize how much they meant to her?

"Yes." Flynn reached out and took her hands in his.

His touch was warm, and her eyes widened as he fell to his knees on the cold, cavernous floor. She breathed his name, but he did not get up.

From his knees, Flynn met her gaze. "Octavia, I have been an ass." He paused as if he was waiting for her to say something, but she would not argue with him. He had been terrible. When he seemed to realize she wasn't going to say anything, he continued, "I'm so sorry."

Her eyes searched his. He seemed truly remorseful, and she wanted to believe that he regretted his actions. "You hurt me." Her voice was soft, and the last word cracked. "I want to believe you. I want this. But how do I know you won't do it again?"

His grip tightened on her fingers. "Please let me make this up to you," he breathed. "Let me prove to you I won't betray you ever again. I know I made mistakes and lied, but if you give me another chance, I vow to spend every single day proving myself to you. I will never lie or try to steal from you again. You have my word, as much as it's worth."

"Flynn—"

"Please let me finish," he asked.

She drew in a breath and nodded. "Alright."

"Octavia, I knew you were special the second we met in the

cabin. Your aura called to me, and I never should've endangered what we had. I will forever regret trying to steal the rose. If you give me another chance, I will never, ever betray you again." He pressed a kiss to her knuckles. "As much as my word is worth, that is my promise to you."

He fell silent then, and so did she. Her heart was beating a thunderous drum as she studied him. Gods, she wanted to believe him. Wanted to forgive him. Wanted *him*.

She just had one question. "Do you regret kissing me when we were with the werewolves?"

"Fuck, no," he said instantly. "I could never regret that. I may regret the actions that I took, but I will never, not in a million years, regret you, Octavia."

Kydona help her, but Octavia believed him. She stared at this man on his knees before her, at the emotions in his eyes, and made up her mind.

"Do you promise you'll never try to steal from me again?" She cocked a brow. "A dragon always knows how many coins they have."

He shook his head. "Never. I'll never betray you again." He shifted to one knee, drawing his sword. Keeping the blade pointed to the ground, he pressed his forehead against the hilt. "I swear to you on my family's steel, if you give me your heart, I will guard it with my sword, my magic, and my soul."

Gods. Not only was he incredibly good-looking, but Flynn was damn good at apologizing, too. The sight of a groveling male on his knees was far more appealing than Octavia ever thought it would be.

She wouldn't keep him waiting. Not now. Not after everything else they'd already been through. She reached down and placed her hands on top of his. He looked up, his eyes gleaming as they met hers. "Please stand," she murmured.

He quickly rose to his feet, sheathing his sword. He remained silent, though, leaving the decision firmly up to her.

Octavia drew in a deep breath and whispered, "I forgive you."

Life was too short to hold onto grudges, especially with Flynn. *My fated mate*, she thought.

She'd never expected this to happen. It was rare, but not unheard of, for mating bonds to exist between species. Octavia would be damned if she gave hers up because of a mistake.

Kydona only knew she'd made more than a few of those over the course of her lifetime.

His eyes widened for a moment before a beaming grin spread across his face. Joy radiated off him, and right then, she knew she'd made the right decision.

Flynn wet his lips, his fingers clenching and unclenching at his sides. "I want to kiss you, Octavia," he breathed. "May I?"

She didn't even pretend to consider his request. "Yes," she murmured. "Please do."

She'd barely said the last word before his mouth crashed into hers. They both stumbled back.

This kiss was different from the others they'd shared. Deeper. Longer. More passionate. It was filled with thankfulness and relief. Every sweep of his lips over hers, every moment they kissed, was better than the last.

Octavia moaned. She couldn't help it. This was, by far, the best kiss she'd ever had in her entire life. Flynn moved his mouth over hers with the precision of someone who knew how to kiss and did it well. One hand landed on her hip, the warmth of his flesh searing through her tunic. The other laced through her hair as he angled her head just so. He kept kissing her even as he walked them back towards the couch.

This kiss was a claiming. A declaration. A promise.

The back of her knees hit the couch, and Flynn's lips moved from hers. He kissed her jaw as his fingers found the hem of her tunic. He rasped, "May I take this off?"

"Of course." Need coursed through her. It felt like a spark had been lit the moment she and Flynn first met, and it had been steadily growing since then. Now that she'd forgiven him, the spark had transformed into a burning fire.

She needed him.

Octavia raised her arms, and Flynn reverently pulled the garment over her head. She hadn't replaced the band around her breasts earlier, a decision which she was thankful for now.

The witch's gaze darkened with pure, primal hunger as he drank in the sight of her. She loved the way he looked at her, loved the need reflected in his eyes, loved the growl that rolled through his chest at the sight of her. The way Flynn looked at Octavia was doing wonders for her self-esteem. She'd never hated the way she looked, but no one had ever made her feel as good as the witch did right now.

"Good gods, Octavia," he rasped, dropping the tunic. "You're so fucking beautiful."

The way he looked at her made her feel like a goddess of seduction, and she loved it. A cool breeze blew into the cave, causing her nipples to pebble.

Feeling uncharacteristically shy, she fought the urge to cover her bare breasts. "Do you think so?"

"I know so," he said with conviction. His hands cradled her cheeks, and he kissed her again. She couldn't help but melt against him. When his lips lifted off hers, he hooked his thumbs into the waistband of her leggings. "May I take these off?"

She was already halfway naked. Why not finish the job?

She nodded, and he kneeled in front of her once again. He kissed her legs, slowly tugging the material down. With each meeting of his mouth against her flesh, the self-consciousness she'd been feeling dissipated. By the time he directed her to step out of her leggings, she was filled with an intense feeling of rightness.

Octavia stood bare before Flynn as he returned to his feet, his gaze sweeping over her. "No man has ever been as lucky as I am right now," he said huskily.

She tugged on his tunic. "I think you're a little overdressed for the occasion."

"Ah." His eyes twinkled, catching the light of the glowing

mushrooms. "I suppose that's true. Allow me to rectify the situation."

He reached behind him and grabbed the back of his tunic, pulling it over his neck in a smooth movement.

Octavia's mouth dried, and her legs wobbled. She sat, grateful for the couch behind her. Between the glowing lights and the hoard's golden glimmer, Flynn looked like... well, like a god. His chest was sculpted, and he was muscular but not bulky. A scar ran diagonally from his left shoulder to the middle of his chest, giving him a distinguished look. And then her gaze dropped even lower, following the V of his abs. There was a defined bulge that had her licking her lips.

Yes, stopping here for the night had definitely been a good idea.

"What about your pants?" she asked, her voice raspier than it had been a moment ago.

Flynn moved towards her with a gleam in his eyes. For a moment, she forgot which one of them was the predator because he looked like he wanted to eat her. The more she thought about that, the more she realized she didn't have a problem with that at all.

What could she say? She found his apology compelling and attractive.

"I'll get to them." He kneeled on the couch, one leg on either side of her, and slowly lowered his head. His lips hovered over hers, and his breath was warm as he whispered, "Eventually."

She inhaled sharply, and he kissed her again. They became a tangle of tongues and teeth as he kissed her until she was hot all over, the heat having started in her core and spiraled through her entire body.

The witch didn't stop there. He kissed a trail down Octavia's neck, nipping and sucking along the way. His cock pressed against her core, already incredibly hard.

Gods, she couldn't wait to get her hands on it.

Octavia reached out to touch him, but he grabbed her hands and held her wrists above her head.

"Careful, beautiful," he purred. "Not yet."

She stared at him through hooded eyes. She could pull her hands back if she wanted to... but she didn't.

Flynn released her hands, dipping his head as he cupped her breasts. "Gods, your skin is so warm," he murmured against her before drawing her nipple into his mouth. He did something with his tongue that sent bolts of pleasure through Octavia.

"Dragon," she half-moaned, half-screamed as his hands continued their carnal, torturous path. "Hot."

He made a sound of approval, releasing her breast before moving to the other one. The wonderful torture continued until Octavia was writhing beneath him, calling his name. The air in the cave thickened and grew heavy with the scents of their mutual desire.

"Flynn, please," she moaned as he continued his trail of kisses. The space between her thighs was soaked, and she shifted her hips, seeking the friction she so desperately needed.

Thank Kydona, the witch moved. His knees landed on the cavern floor as he kissed and licked his way down her stomach to her thighs. He was everywhere but where Octavia wanted him. Her words were a babble of pleas as he paid attention to every part of her except where she needed him most.

Eventually, Flynn paused his pleasurable assault, kissing her inner thigh. A deep chuckle hummed in his chest. "What do you want, Octavia?"

She growled, "You know what I want." There was no way someone could kiss as well as he did and be oblivious to the ways of the world.

Then his hands skated right over her sensitive core, grazing that one spot where she needed him most. It was all the confirmation she needed—he knew exactly what he was doing. "I need to hear you say it." His breath danced over her clit, and her core spiraled tighter, tighter, tighter.

"Oh gods, please," Octavia begged him. "Just touch me already."

Was the last chuckle dark? This one rumbled through him like a roll of thunder. "With pleasure, beautiful."

Not even a heartbeat later, his mouth landed on her. He nipped and sucked at her clit until she was nothing but a puddle beneath him. She laced her fingers through his hair, holding him there as her head fell back against the couch.

"Use your words, Octavia," he murmured against her. "Tell me what you want."

Speaking had never been as difficult as it was at that moment. "More," she begged him, her eyes slipping shut. "I don't want you to stop."

"Good girl." He returned to her sensitive flesh, and this time, he slipped a finger inside her.

She groaned, biting her lip. Pleasure was a coursing river running through her. There was a cliff, and she was so close to careening right off the edge.

Flynn knew. Another finger joined the first, and he crooked them in a beckoning motion, bringing her closer and closer to her release. That connection between them hummed with approval as she moaned beneath him.

If he stopped now, she would die. She just knew it.

She held him in place, letting each kiss and lick and thrust of his fingers carry her to the precipice of oblivion. And when she tumbled over the edge, her scream echoed off the walls of the cavern. Her eyes fluttered shut, and pleasure ripped through her.

Flynn kept touching her through her climax, his touch now gentle and his kisses soft as the waves slowly receded.

Octavia had never experienced anything close to this in all her years. The partners she'd had before had *never* been able to make her feel like that.

Eventually, she reopened her eyes. At some point, Flynn had removed the remainder of his clothes. He stood naked before her, a purely masculine look of pride on his face.

Her gaze traveled down, down, down, stopping at his hardened length.

She licked her lips, wanting to taste him as he had tasted her. She wanted to feel him come apart in her mouth.

Octavia must have said the words out loud because Flynn laughed quietly and shook his head. "Another time, beautiful." He stepped towards her. In a movement that was at once powerful and gentle, he lifted her from the couch and swapped their places.

This time, Octavia straddled him. Flynn's hardness rubbed up against her, and a groan slipped from her lips. "I want you." She leaned in to kiss him as she wantonly rubbed herself against him. "All of you."

It didn't matter that they'd only known each other for a short time, didn't matter how they'd started, because right now, she couldn't imagine being anywhere else in the world.

He kissed her back. "Gods, I want you, too."

She shifted her hips, rubbing the tip of his cock with her wetness. If she were in a playful mood, she'd tease him, but right now, her need was so strong that she could think of nothing else but having him.

Instead, she slanted her mouth over his. Flynn gripped her hips. His touch was firm but not bruising.

Octavia slowly lowered herself onto his cock. He was... big. Far larger than Octavia was used to. His hands tightened around her as she moved slowly until she took him to the hilt.

His head fell back, and sweat beaded on his forehead. "Fuck, you're so tight."

Octavia couldn't reply. Nothing could've prepared her for this. Her heart hammered as she grew accustomed to him. He didn't move, instead letting her get used to his size.

Eventually, she lifted her hips. Her mouth opened in a breathless gasp as pain and pleasure shot through her. It had been so long. Too long, apparently.

Concern filled Flynn's gaze as he leaned forward. He brushed his lips over hers. "Take your time."

She did. She tried again, and this time, it felt better. He was patient, murmuring sweet, gentle nothings in her ear as he let her set the pace. His thrusts were patient and slow... until she was ready for more.

"Harder," she murmured, kissing his neck. "Please."

He didn't need any other encouragement. His fingers gripped her hips, and he thrust upwards, slamming into her. She cried out, the sound filled with pleasure as he hit exactly the right spot within her.

He groaned.

She moaned.

Together, they drew nearer and nearer to the edge of oblivion. The pain was long gone, a distant memory lost as pleasure crested within her once again. His hand slipped between them, and he rubbed her clit.

A strangled sound that was half-scream, half-plea for more came from her mouth.

He captured the sound, slanting his lips over hers.

They were two, but they moved together as one. She gasped as he hit that spot inside her.

"Close," she whispered. "So close."

She could feel oblivion drawing nearer, nearer, nearer.

He rasped, "I want to see you come on my cock."

Those words catapulted Octavia over the cliff. She cried out, trembling as pleasure raced through her. He quickly followed her, his release filling her up.

Octavia panted, her chest heaving against his. "Wow," she said after she caught her breath. "That was..."

"Incredible." He captured her mouth with his again, this kiss languid and slow.

"It really was." She smiled, shifting so she was no longer on his lap, and settled her head on his shoulder. "You know, I think you might have just ruined sex for me with anyone else."

Nothing would ever compare to this.

A moment passed before Flynn threw back his head and roared with laughter. The sound echoed around the cave. "Is that so?"

It most certainly was. Octavia pretended to consider for just a moment before nodding. "Yes, I believe so."

A lazy grin spread across Flynn's face. "Well, in that case, I certainly wouldn't want to leave you wanting." He trailed a hand down her chest, his gaze growing hungry as he studied her. "Again?"

Octavia spread her legs, testing the soreness between her thighs. She was a dragon and already healing. Besides, they had all night. She couldn't think of anything else she'd rather be doing.

She reached out, gripping his already hardening length. "Again."

CHAPTER 11
An Exchange is Made

The air in the southernmost region of the Rose Empire was so dry that Octavia felt like her scales were cracking. Despite having stopped for water before she took off, she was parched. The sun, though not at its peak, beat down on her and dried her out even further.

So far, Octavia did not love Sandhaven.

She and Flynn had stayed awake until the early morning hours, but she was *not* complaining. By the time they'd fallen asleep in a tangle of limbs on the couch, they were both sated and limp with delight. As predicted, she had been sore when she woke, but it had been undeniably worth it. They'd gathered the necessary provisions for rescuing Amyla and washed up in a nearby stream before Octavia had shifted. Flynn had climbed on, and she'd taken to the skies.

It was time to save Flynn's sister. The question of their mating bond remained in the back of Octavia's mind as they flew, and she pondered it. Neither of them had brought it up last night, but she couldn't deny the connection that existed between them. Octavia thought she knew what she wanted to do, but first, they had to get to Sandhaven safely.

Even though she'd never been there, she knew where she was

going. All dragon shifters studied the geography of the Rose Empire as part of their schooling as children. It was important, after all, since they could be sent all over the Empire to deliver missives.

The continent was massive. The north was snowy and frozen, filled with icy lakes and mountains that stretched towards the Black Sea. The land in the west was flat. Wheat and other grains grew in the west, providing much-needed sustenance to the citizens of the Empire. In the east, forests and mountains were spread as far as the eye could see. And the south? Deserts. Sand, sand, and more sand.

Like a yellow ocean, the tiny grains stretched from one point of the horizon to the other. The land wasn't flat, as Octavia had expected. Dunes rose like small golden hills, reflecting the brilliance of the sun. Though she didn't see any creatures, she knew they were there. She could sense them, just as much as they could probably sense her.

The difference was that in this form, Octavia was the biggest predator around. No one would bother them... at least until she shifted so they could deal with the thugs who had Flynn's sister.

That could potentially be a problem.

Hopefully, the gods would be on their side.

What will you do if the witchling isn't there? the dragon asked.

I don't know. Octavia banked her wings, turning to the right. *Hopefully, she is.*

She was invested in this now. Not just because she'd given Flynn the money from the rose and her hoard but because she was intrigued. What kind of woman must Amyla be to inspire her brother to go to such lengths to help her?

It wasn't long before the landscape shifted. Structures rose from the sand, dotting the horizon. Long, tall buildings with wooden roofs stood like sentries among the golden ocean, their presence incongruous with the never-ending desert.

A city in the sand.

Flynn gripped Octavia's neck and shouted for his voice to be heard over the flapping of her wings. "There! The tallest building on the right."

At the edge of Sandhaven, visible even from here, the building he pointed to stood out like a sore thumb. A beacon of darkness and trouble, it was a giant among its peers. Even from here, an aura of wrongness surrounded it.

Of course, that was their destination.

Tilting her wings, Octavia let the air guide her closer to the ground. They'd already decided that she would shift before they got too close to town. After that, they'd approach the rest of the way on foot. It would be safer that way. They didn't want to spook the people holding Amyla.

Landing inside a grove of palm trees, Octavia waited until Flynn slipped off her back before she pulled on her shift. Returning to herself was easy, the pain barely there as she slipped out of her dragon form and into her two-legged one. By the time she was back on her feet, Flynn had withdrawn her tunic and leggings from the messenger bag.

He handed them to Octavia, but he didn't let go. Instead, he drew her in for a kiss. "I stand by my earlier assessment."

"Oh?" She raised a brow, not minding that she remained naked.

"You are gorgeous," he murmured against her lips. "Amazing in both forms."

Blood rushed to her cheeks, and she grinned as she dressed. "Thank you." She studied him, her gaze sweeping from his wind-kissed hair and sword hanging on his back. "You don't look so bad yourself."

A deep laugh rumbled through him as he handed her the messenger bag, and the coins clinked together as she slid it over her shoulder. Then, he gave her the walking stick he'd strapped to his back before they left.

"Ready?" He laced their hands together, the movement so natural it was as though they'd been together for years.

Her chest hummed at their closeness, and she tightened her grip on her walking stick. "Ready."

WALKING IN THE DESERT, even for a short period of time, was far less enjoyable than flying above it. By the time they reached Sandhaven, sweat was pouring down Octavia's flesh in rivulets. Not only that, but the bottle of water they'd filled in the spring before leaving was down to its last drops.

They needed to find Amyla and get out of there quickly. The only good thing was that Octavia's ankle wasn't bothering her today. It was a small mercy, but it did make the rest of the conditions a little more bearable.

At least Flynn had his sword. The closer they got to Sandhaven, the more thankful she was for the weapon. Though Sandhaven appeared warm and welcoming for the most part, they were headed to a part of town that reeked of danger. Businesses didn't grow here, markets didn't flourish, and people's lives weren't happy.

The sooner they could leave, the better.

Flynn's grip on Octavia's hand tightened as he led her through increasingly narrow streets. Earlier, children's laughter could be heard as they passed happy family homes and businesses, but that was no longer the case. This place was too silent. The air was too dry. Their footsteps were too loud.

Death resided in this place.

We shouldn't linger here, the dragon warned Octavia.

She wholeheartedly agreed with the creature. The sooner they got out of here, the better.

Octavia's skin crawled, and she was on high alert as they strode through the empty streets of Sandhaven. It was midday. People should be here. The streets were like graveyards.

Wrong, wrong, wrong.

Thank the gods, they finally reached the building. White walls stretched to the sky, and it was several stories higher than any other structure around.

"This is the place?" Octavia wished she'd brought a dagger with her instead of just her walking stick.

"It is." Flynn nodded, his shoulders tense. Blue sparks danced over his hands, and he was stiff. "Let me do the talking."

That wouldn't be a problem. Octavia didn't have a death wish, and she knew the value of holding her tongue. She said as much to Flynn, and he snorted before raising his fist and knocking.

The sound barely had time to resonate before the door was wrenched open.

A towering male with greasy brown hair stood before them, violence flickering in his eyes as he glowered at them. "Yes?" he said in the Common Tongue, his words clipped and deep as though he was eating rocks.

Yeah, Octavia definitely didn't plan to speak with this man.

Flynn lifted his chin. "I'm here for Amyla Tririver."

A grumble ran through the man, predatory and animalistic and deep. Octavia's dragon stood on edge, the predator within her ready to come out if needed.

The burly man stared at them for a long moment, his jaw clenched so tight a vein popped. Eventually, he nodded curtly. "Come."

THE INTERIOR of the building was even worse than the exterior. The silence was more oppressive. The aura of wrongness was even thicker. Octavia felt like they were wading through mud.

Danger was here.

She kept her senses extended, ready to act if needed. Beside her, Flynn flexed his fingers. He hadn't drawn his sword, but his hand rested on the hilt.

Neither of them was at peace.

The hulking man led them up a set of wooden stairs and down

a hallway. They trailed him through a common area with a few ripped couches, where several women wearing little more than undergarments sat and read.

Or at least it looked like they were reading. No one spoke. No one moved. They just stared at the books with dead eyes, not even turning the pages.

Wrong, wrong, wrong.

Octavia shivered and pressed herself against Flynn's side. This was not a place for her—it was not a place for any of these women. Suddenly, she wished they'd brought all the money from her hoard. How much would it cost to free all these women? Once they freed Amyla, she vowed they would come back for the others. Maybe not today or tomorrow, but they would free them.

No one should be forced to live in a place like this.

A few minutes later, Flynn was forced to repeat his request to see his sister in front of another man. This one had a scar running down half his face, his left eye cloudy as he glared at them.

"You wish to buy my property?" he snarled, his voice low and rough. His fingers dug into the desk in front of him.

Flynn stiffened, and Octavia could tell it took every ounce of restraint the witch had not to tremble with fury. "Yes," he said through clenched teeth. "I do."

That silence stretched and stretched and stretched as the man looked them over. Then, he raised a brow. "Fine. You want her?" He named a price. "That's how much it will cost."

Flynn's knuckles whitened. They had just enough.

Octavia's heart was a thundering drum growing louder as the minutes went by. Flynn spoke with the man, but she barely heard their words. The longer they were in this place, the worse she felt. They needed to leave.

Eventually, the scarred man stood, walked to the door, and barked an order. He turned in the doorway, his form looming over them, and he stared them down.

Wrong, wrong, wrong.

Every second they spent in this place was worse than the last.

The walls bore down on Octavia, and the silence was almost too much to bear. Her dragon was anxious and itchy beneath her skin, her lungs too tight.

She needed to get out of here.

It felt like hours passed before the door opened again. A petite woman stood in the threshold, shaking hands gripping a dress that had seen far better days. Her long reddish-brown hair was the same shade as Flynn's, and her wide eyes were frozen in shock.

Flynn crossed the room and pulled the woman in for a hug.

"Amyla," he breathed into her hair, holding her to him.

The young woman stood frozen in his arms as if she couldn't believe what was happening. "Flynn?" His name was little more than a whisper on her lips.

"Yes." He kissed the top of her head. "I'm here."

Those final words seemed to thaw whatever ice held the girl in place. A sob burst from her lips, and she buried her face in her brother's chest.

"You came, you came, you came." The words were quieter each time, more broken, until they were nothing but whimpers on Amyla's lips.

Tears burned in Octavia's eyes, and her chest was tight.

This was so beautiful, so right, and she'd played a part in it. It didn't bother her that she'd parted with some of her gold, nor did it bother her that Flynn had tried to steal from her because right now, they'd freed a young woman from a terrible fate.

After a few minutes, Flynn looked up and met her gaze. *Thank you*, his eyes seemed to say. *For this. For my sister.*

And as she smiled back, despite their awful surroundings, a peace settled upon her.

The connection remained between her and Flynn. It thrummed with life, as it had ever since their night together. The mating question had been in the back of her mind all day, but now, she knew what she would do.

CHAPTER 12
Peace Comes in Many Forms

O ctavia's dragon swooped low, the thatched roofs of Fallton coming into view as she flew through the clouds.

After the rescue yesterday, they'd flown from Sandhaven to Thyr, a growing city in the middle of the Rose Empire. After a quiet night in The Rosebud, an inn on the edge of town, they'd taken to the skies once again. Octavia and Flynn hadn't had the chance to talk last night. The witch had spent the night conversing quietly with his sister before she'd fallen asleep in his arms. It hadn't seemed right to interrupt, so Octavia had kept her decision to herself.

Octavia's two riders held on tight to her back. Initially, Octavia had suggested that she drop Flynn and Amyla off on the edge of town, letting them go to their family together, but Flynn insisted that Octavia come with them. He wanted to introduce her to his family.

Nerves fluttered around in her stomach like tiny butterflies. No one had ever taken Octavia home to meet their family. No one had ever cared enough. Hopefully, she wouldn't make a fool of herself. She had grown rather comfortable with the witch over the past few days, but meeting his family was an entirely different matter.

Octavia roared, banking her wings as she descended towards the cobblestone town square. It was midday, and there were several groups of people milling about. She didn't try to hide. Instead, she let her size and color catch their attention. It wasn't difficult. Bright purple dragons were not inconspicuous.

Screams and shouts of amazement filled the air as Octavia circled the square. She remained in the air, waiting until there was no one in the square before landing. Her descent was smooth and easy as if she'd done it hundreds of times before. Her talons gripped the stones, and her tail thumped on the ground. From her back slid the two witches.

Moments later, Flynn circled around to Octavia's front. Her walking stick and his sword were strapped to his back. He held her clothes in one hand and placed the other hand on her nose.

"Thank you, beautiful." His forehead pressed against her snout. "I'll never be able to repay you."

Octavia frowned. Or she would have, but dragons couldn't really frown. She would have to talk to him about that, though. He didn't owe her anything. For one, she'd only done what any decent person would do. Anyone who had seen the place where Amyla was being held would know that it was not suitable for any person. But perhaps more importantly, there was no debt between them because she could never hold her mate in that kind of position.

They didn't have time to talk about that, though, because a high-pitched squeal came from nearby. A woman wearing a long walnut brown dress came running between two wattle and daub houses, wiping her hands on her flour-dusted apron. A white braid flew behind her, and her cheeks were ruddy as tears ran down her face.

"Amyla," the woman sobbed. She gathered the witchling in her arms and wept.

Flynn leaned against Octavia's hind leg. "My mother," he murmured, running his hand down her scales.

Yes, Octavia had gathered as much.

After that, four other young women and an older man quickly followed. The rest of Flynn's family. There was a flurry of tears and hugs and joyful reuniting. It was a beautiful scene.

Flynn eventually left his post, joining his family and recounting the tale of his sister's rescue. There were more hugs, more tears, more love.

Octavia was starting to feel bad about intruding on this obviously personal moment when Flynn turned back to her. The smile on his face could only be described as glowing as he strode over and placed a hand on her scales. "Mother, Father. I'd like to introduce you to someone very special to me." He turned to Octavia. "Will you shift?"

She huffed a reply and nodded. Flynn stepped back, holding her clothes, as his family turned their backs. The moment of privacy was appreciated as Octavia pulled on her magic. That white light flashed, and by the time she was back on her two legs, he was already handing her clothes.

It was like they had done this a thousand times before.

She dressed quickly, not wanting to flash Flynn's entire village, before pressing a kiss to his cheek. "Thank you," she murmured.

He smiled. "Thank you. Are you ready to meet my family?"

Well, even if she wasn't, it wasn't like she could say no. They were already here. Luckily, she was eager to make their acquaintance. "I am."

Slinging his arm over her shoulders, Flynn held Octavia close as he led her over to the family. When they were close, he asked them to turn around.

"Mama, Papa, I'd like to introduce you to someone special," he said. "This is Octavia Ashbloom." He paused, then added, "My mate."

Hearing those words sent a rush of heat through Octavia. She grinned.

She had a mate, and it was... good.

If Octavia had thought that Flynn's family was loud before, that was nothing compared to their reaction now. She had never heard someone squeal as loudly as Flynn's mother did at that moment. The woman ran over and wrapped her arms around Octavia.

"Oh my gods," she exclaimed. "A mate! You're goddess-blessed, both of you." She gasped, clutching her hands over her heart. "This is incredible. You know, we never..."

A stream of words exploded from the older witch as she led Octavia to their home. The dragon shifter didn't even have the chance to respond, and to be honest, she didn't even try. This reception was far more than she had ever anticipated.

If Octavia had returned to Firefall, she was certain that the other dragons would have been lukewarm towards her at best. Perhaps even hurtful. But here? In this place, with her mate and his family? There wasn't a hint of that to be found.

No, as she entered the homey three-bedroom cottage that housed Flynn's family, the only thing Octavia felt was love. She soon learned most of his sisters lived with their families in houses nearby, but Flynn and Amyla still resided with their parents.

It was loud, but somehow, it didn't bother Octavia. Everyone was going out of their way to make her comfortable, and she appreciated it more than she could express.

The day flew by. Octavia didn't have a moment alone to talk to Flynn because there were so many people. So much laughter. Tears. Joy. He had to recount the story of Amyla's rescue a dozen times as more and more friends and extended family stopped by.

Each time someone new came, Flynn introduced her in the same way. "This is Octavia Ashbloom. My mate."

Whenever he said the words, that connection between them thrummed. He did not leave her side, somehow knowing that she did not want to be left alone in this place where she knew no one else. His hand was sturdy in hers, and he didn't let her stand for long before a stool magically appeared.

It seemed impossible that Flynn could be even more handsome, but he was positively glowing, surrounded by his family.

They ate a delicious meal of stew and fresh bread prepared by Flynn's mother, and then the family gathered around an outdoor campfire under the stars.

It was cool but not cold, and the crackling fire kept everyone warm. Stories were shared, mostly Flynn's family telling Octavia all about the mischief he got up to as a child, and laughter rang through the night. Eventually, the family trickled inside until only Octavia and Flynn remained.

They sat side by side, their hands linked as the silence of the night surrounded them. Octavia's head rested on Flynn's shoulder, and she felt... at peace.

Eventually, Flynn's thumb brushed against Octavia's knuckles. "You seem like you're deep in thought."

Octavia's lips twitched, and she looked up at him. "I am."

She'd been thinking ever since their night in the cave.

"Do you care to fill me in on those thoughts?"

She wanted to. Honestly, she'd wanted to tell him the moment she came to the decision. But the moments earlier hadn't been right.

But now... this was the moment she'd been waiting for.

Taking in a deep, fortifying breath, she turned to him. This was it. "I want to accept the mating bond," she breathed. "I mean, we don't have to do it right now, and if you're not sure, I'm happy to wait. But I've made my decision. I want you. All of you."

The decision was quick, yes, but it wasn't rash. Octavia was Mature. She'd lived for several decades, and she knew what she wanted. Seeing Flynn with his family had cemented the decision she'd reached earlier—she wanted their bond.

His eyes widened in surprise. "You do?"

She dipped her chin. "I do. I mean, if you—"

"Yes. It's not even a question." He released her hands, only to cup her cheeks instead. "I've felt the bond since the moment we first met. Of course, I want it." His eyes searched hers. "I want you, Octavia."

He tugged her to her feet, and his hands fell around her waist. He held her close, the snapping fire at their backs as he lowered his head.

"You're mine," he whispered, sounding like he could barely believe it.

"I'm yours, and you're mine," Octavia breathed just as he slanted his lips over hers.

The fire was their witness as they kissed beneath the stars, affirming their decision. That sense of rightness bloomed into a beautiful flower in Octavia's soul. When she'd left Firefall, she never guessed this would be waiting for her in the wilds of the Rose Empire.

And yet, she wouldn't have it any other way.

Later that night, when they bound themselves together in the sacred mating ceremony, peace settled deep within Octavia.

The emerald rose had brought them together, and now, nothing would ever break them apart.

THE END

THANK YOU FOR COMING ALONG WITH OCTAVIA AND FLYNN ON THEIR JOURNEY TO THEIR HAPPY ENDING.

Reviews mean the world to indie authors like me. If you enjoyed this story, it would mean the world to me if you could leave one.

Not finished with me yet? You can explore this world in The Binding Chronicles, The Ithenmyr Chronicles, and The Choosing Chronicles.

Come hang out with me and my readers on Facebook! Join Elayna R. Gallea's Reader Group

Acknowledgments

We made it! I hope you enjoyed Octavia and Flynn's story as much as I did. Journeying back to the Rose Empire and exploring the world before the Four Kingdoms and the Republic of Balance was so much fun, and I enjoyed exploring the continent from Octavia's point of view.

To my husband, Aaron, thank you for your unending support. This book wouldn't exist without you.

To my alpha and beta readers, thank you for reading this story in its raw form. Your feedback helped make the story what it is today.

To my writer's group, thank you for listening when I come to you with crazy ideas.

And to you, my reader. Thank you for being here, entering my worlds, and reading my stories.

Without you, none of this would be possible.

From the bottom of my heart, thank you.

Elayna

Also by Elayna R. Gallea

The Choosing Chronicles

A Game of Love and Betrayal

A Heart of Desire and Deceit

The Binding Chronicles (*A high fantasy arranged marriage vampire romance series in the Four Kingdoms*)

Tethered

Tormented

Treasured

Troubled

The Ithenmyr Chronicles (*An interconnected series that takes place in the Four Kingdoms at the same time as Tethered*)

Of Earth and Flame

Of Wings and Briars

Of Ash and Ivy

Of Thistles and Talons

Of Shale and Smoke

Legends of Love (New Adult Standalones)

A Court of Fire and Frost (a Romeo and Juliet Retelling)

A Court of Seas and Storms (a Little Mermaid Retelling)

A Court of Wind and Wings (a Hades and Persephone Retelling)

The Sequencing Chronicles (Young Adult) - a complete series

Sequenced

Rise of the Subversives

The Wielder of Prophecy

The Runaway Healer (a prequel novella)

About the Author

Elayna R. Gallea lives in beautiful New Brunswick, Canada with her husband and two children. They live in the land of snow and forests in the Saint John River Valley.

When Elayna isn't living in her head, she can be found toiling around her house watching Food Network, listening to broadway, and planning her next meal.

Elayna enjoys copious amounts of chocolate, cheese, and wine. Not in that order.

You can find her making a fool of herself on Tiktok and Instagram on a daily basis.

Printed in Great Britain
by Amazon

54276790R00078